WHAT PEOPLE ARE SAYING ABOUT THE HOUSE ON PRYTANIA.

Pat Carr's fiction opens a window onto the hidden lives of characters who might seem familiar at first glance: the corporate attorney aiming for a cheap settlement, the luckless young woman sewing sleeves in a factory, the disabled mother imagining herself strong, graceful, and lovely. The impressions her stories offer are brief—a handful of pages spanning a few days or hours—but by the time the people they've allowed you to glimpse vanish back into the privacy of their lives, you'll realize how much depth their experiences contain, how much mystery, and how little you knew them in the first place. Carr writes deftly, unobtrusively, and humanely, and there's never any question where her sympathies lie.—Kevin Brockmeier, author of *The Brief History of the Dead*

The House on Prytania, a collection both compelling and beautifully crafted, presents a variety of believable voices that tell stories of betrayal, fear, conviction and hope. This may be my favorite Pat Carr short story collection.—Angela Leone, author of *Swimming toward the Light*

These stories show wryness reminiscent of de Maupassant and many have a sting in the tail like O. Henry's. Set in the South, mainly Louisiana and Arkansas, but the real South, devoid of stereotypes and sentimentality, like the best of Ellen Gilchrist, this collection will move you, surprise you, and amuse you. Who said literary fiction cannot be entertaining? Pat Carr knows that it can and should. Here is a writer on top of her form, whose attention to detail, imagery, compassion and irony will delight you. But I give you fair warning: you will find *The House on Prytania* impossible to put down.—Garry Craig Powell, author of *Stoning the Devil*

D1520329

THE HOUSE ON PRYTANIA

...and other stories from the South

To Pam, with all my love,
Pat Carr

THE HOUSE ON PRYTANIA

...and other stories from the South

BY PAT CARR

HHp

High Hill Press, Missouri

High Hill Press Edition © 2014

Cover created by High Hill Press
Inside layout by High Hill Press

First Edition 1 2 3 4 5 6 7 8 9 10

ISBN: 978-1-60653-081-8
Library of Congress Number in Publication Data

High Hill Press Missouri USA
HighHillPress@aol.com

To Leona Epstein and Judith Gabbard, with all my love

THE HOUSE ON PRYTANIA

Mrs. Parrish wasn't my mother, and that was probably why I could see it and Lily couldn't.

Or so I thought at the time.

It was only later I understood that perhaps Lily had been aware and that even Mr. Parrish may have pretended he hadn't noticed. He always made conventional—stiff and meaningless—remarks, beaming, as if it was entirely logical to come home at two in the afternoon to find us, Lily and me and Mrs. Parrish in the kitchen around the big oak table, laughing and joking with Armond.

I'd known, even at eleven, that my mother wouldn't have sat in any room with Armond. Not that she was prejudiced. She always pointedly showed her Garden District listings to black professionals when other agents in her office refused or feigned too busy a schedule. It was just that she couldn't have thought of anything to say to her gardener-carpenter after she'd decided what shade of maroon she wanted the gutters painted or where she wanted the flat of peonies bedded. She hired workmen for competent jobs, and if Armond had been her handyman, she'd have expected him to change the light fixtures and caulk the tub before she got home. I couldn't imagine her hovering at the foot of a ladder, bracing the toolbox or dispensing screw-drivers as he needed them.

Which may have been what gave me the first, not-quite-conscious clue.

"You've been working here how long?" I asked him one afternoon. I wouldn't have been that brash with any other adult, but this was Armond, and we were sitting at the table while Mrs. Parrish fried beignets for the four of us.

"Let's see, how long, Eva?" He looked at Mrs. Parrish. "Since I was seventeen or eighteen I guess. Since Lily must've been about two."

He seemed older than twenty-six, with silver coiling like fine sterling wire through his black sideburns and an incisor replaced and glinting old-man-gold when he laughed.

"Mason said I could buy this ante-bellum white elephant if I'd guarantee he never had to hear a word about repairs and never had to lift a finger to do any of them." Mrs. Parrish waved her slotted frying spoon and grease sparkled onto the floor. One reason for going to Lily's was that her mother talked to us as if we were capable of understanding ordinary conversation. "So when this skinny teen-ager showed up at the State Street house and had the audacity to say the north side was peeling and he'd only charge $500 to scrape it and repaint, I told him not to move. I ran in, called your mother, and told her to draw up the papers on this place. I knew he'd been sent from Heaven."

"Don't blaspheme, Eva," he said sharply. Then he reached out to douse the fresh batch of beignets with powdered sugar while he dropped the frown and grinned at Mrs. Parrish. "Of course I didn't know what I was getting myself into. A board flaps loose or a brick dislodges somewhere on these old houses every day. You'd have a pile of rubble on this lot in no time if you didn't keep after it."

I recognized exaggeration when I heard it. Especially since my mother always said that Garden District houses stayed in remarkably good shape considering the Louisiana climate, and I remember thinking that Armond Dupin, the back of whose hand was no darker than the tawny puffed beignets and whose great-great-great grandfather had volunteered for the Creole-of-Color Brigade to defend New Orleans in the Civil War, knew a cushy maintenance job when he rang the doorbell on one.

A couple of days later on our way to the attic, where Lily intended to stuff her fat legs into sequined Mardi Gras gowns and pretend to be Queen of Rex, I glanced in the second floor study. Armond and Mrs. Parrish hunched on the rug over a tall shutter laid flat between them, and in the gray rain, I thought their fingers might have been braided together.

"I got to drill new holes for the screws," he was saying, and neither of them looked up as we passed. And Lily just finished what she was telling me about how her daddy would take us in costumes to a Carnival party at the Pontalba when we were twelve.

After a while in the attic, I got cross-eyed ignoring Lily's rolls of flesh bulging through the emerald and purple satin dresses, and I tried to peer out the windows into the cemetery across the street. Silver rain obscured the view of the oven graves too much for me to imagine stories about their occupants, however, and I strolled over to some warped cartons under the eaves.

"Do you like this tiara?" Lily asked behind me.

"Sure." I folded back cardboard flaps as soft as damp leaf mulch. On top lay a mildewed photo album with pages surprisingly brittle.

I turned a few before I came to a snapshot I could tell was Mrs. Parrish decked out in beads and a headband around her long sepia hair. I looked at it and wondered how she ever got together with established New Orleans money like Mason Parrish, but I didn't ask, and instead said, "How old is your mom?"

"Forty-six. Why?"

"I just wondered."

There were, of course, no pictures of Armond.

Rain swirled down the windows, and finally the costumes got tedious even to Lily. "Let's go down and make some macaroni and cheese," she said. "I'm starved."

"I'd rather stay here." I didn't add that macaroni and cheese wasn't my idea of gourmet.

"It only takes twenty minutes to make." She bounced toward the stairs. "I'll go cook it and bring it up on a tray."

"Fine."

I sat down on a rush mat that didn't soften the floor but did give off a sweet dry grass odor to make the attic less moldy. Gray waves slithered across the windows, and I let my eyes glaze while I inched prone on the woven straw.

"—and how you can— more beautiful— every time, girl—"

Parcels of Armond's words nudged up through the floorboards like toast.

"—just more nearsighted, baby." Mrs. Parrish's laugh slid into spaces of the mat.

The master bedroom lay directly below the attic, and they must have assumed both Lily and I were clunking pans in the kitchen.

And suddenly, without analyzing what I knew, I realized I didn't want Lily to find out. I'd become implicated, a third keeper of a secret I hadn't known I already perceived.

I lay on the mat in cramped indecision.

How could I sneak across the ancient floor without squeaking the boards or quaking the bedroom ceiling? How could I reach the kitchen before Lily tromped up the stairs with clotted macaroni and cheese on a tray?

And yet even as I debated how to protect Mrs. Parrish and Armond, my mind saw his bare chest—the golden shade of the cypress box my mother "bought for a song" at an estate sale—pressed against her. I didn't have a picture of her without clothes, but nude images from TV hazed in my head as the bed thumped a wall in the room below.

I heard a throaty hum combined with a closed-mouthed yelp like after you burn yourself and don't want anyone to know. Then a low laugh that could have come from either one or both of them at the same time.

Holding my breath, I giant-stepped to the door under cover of the laugh.

I grabbed the banister and took the stairs two at a time.

I wasn't sure how I felt about being involved in Mrs. Parrish's affair, and I decided to stay away from the house on Prytania for a while. But it was nearly summer and since no one else from my class lived within walking distance, after a few days of telling Lily I had homework, I went back to their kitchen table.

It was the afternoon Armond said his wife Denise wanted to move to Chicago.

"Whatever for?" Mrs. Parrish, pouring coffee from a percolator with one hand and hot milk from a saucepan with the other, jolted the liquids to a stop.

"She keeps telling me I can get as good a job up there as I got here."

I'd seen Armond's wife once when she waited in his panel truck on their way to Wednesday church, a woman with a stern, bitter chocolate face whose bosom put a lot of stress on the seams of her flowered dress, and I could tell from one glance that she didn't have a great-great-great grandfather who'd served in the Creole-of-Color Brigade.

"Chicago's a dangerous city." Mrs. Parrish's blue eyes flickered while she resumed pouring the café-au-lait.

"That's what I tell her, but she says if I don't go with her, one of these days she'll go alone." He pronounced "says" to rhyme with "days."

"Maybe you could try it for a while." She used a reasonable tone, and she set the cups before us with her usual calm, but I could tell she didn't intend to convince him to try Chicago for a while.

"I was born here," he said. "Away from this muggy heat, I'd dry to ashes like that plug of Spanish moss they tried to get started in New York's Central Park." He dumped three heaping spoons of sugar into his cup as he looked at Mrs. Parrish.

And I wasn't surprised to hear that Mrs. Parrish talked her husband into buying a summer place across Lake Ponchartrain. Armond would remodel it for additional income on Saturdays and still have Sundays for his church.

"After the screens are up, I'll take you girls over," Mrs. Parrish said.

She was spending a lot of time across the lake, too, so Lily sat out most weekends at her grandmother's ugly house with its ugly wrought iron grape balcony on St. Ann Street, and it was August before Mrs. P., Armond, Lily and I drove over the Causeway in his panel truck for our outing. Mrs. P. and Armond in the front seat didn't talk much, and Lily pouted because she couldn't see out. I didn't mind missing the Pontchartrain since thirty miles of chopped lake water is pretty lead gray dull, but when we piled out at the summer place, I could tell things weren't going to be much better than the drive.

The ramshackle house was primitive and the yard was overgrown with tobacco-looking plants crowding each other into yellow extinction despite the rain. The exterior paint of the house had eroded too much to guess at a color, and Armond had stacked cinder blocks below the door for temporary steps. Inside, a sway-backed hall led to a couple of bedrooms, a bare living room, and an even emptier kitchen—with yawning spaces for cabinets—and a screened porch.

Mrs. P. had fixed Lily and me a picnic lunch so we could go exploring, and we set off on a desultory tour. But after we finished the sandwiches and blundered into a thicket of blackberry vines, we returned to the house. I noticed at once the uneasiness adding to the heat.

"Go wash your faces and cool off," Mrs. P. said, and although I could tell she meant it to come out cheery, her voice was as stiff as her mouth. She and Armond leaned over coffee cups on a card table, but it was as if they sat across from strangers.

Lily and I went out, siphoned water from the metal jug onto our foreheads and blackberry scratches, and trudged back in with streams dripping off our chins and fingers.

But the air hadn't changed, and Armond was saying, "—can't go on."

Mrs. P.'s hand fluttered toward him as she looked at us. "Anyone for lemonade?"

For dinner, she took a spinach salad from the cooler and produced some shelf cups of Jello for dessert, but Armond ate in silence, and since Lily's pout returned because there wasn't any TV, conversation in the lilac and tangerine sunset was left to Mrs. Parrish and me.

We tried, but since it was only seven when she cleared the paper plates, she said in that pebbled way she'd said everything that evening, "Who wants to play Hearts?"

"That sounds good," I said in the hearty way I'd been saying everything, and I chunked Armond's arm. "Let's be partners."

He glanced up and managed a smile, like he was ashamed of his silent treatment, and said, "We'll skunk them."

We limped through some games of Hearts that no one's was in and lit a kerosene lamp that burned too hot for all of us.

Finally, after a couple of hours, I said, "Man, am I sleepy. Would it be all right if I went to bed?"

"Of course, dear." And I thought I detected appreciation of how I'd been trying.

Lily and I escaped to the bedroom, got into shorty pajamas, and plopped down on a sleeping bag. Within a couple of minutes, Lily was snuffling that snore of hers, but I lay there and realized I could see a slice of light through the door and could hear the conversation from the porch perfectly.

They were discussing wiring and pouring a slab off the kitchen, and they went on for so long I was about to drowse off. But when Armond said clearly, "I want you to get a divorce and marry me," I snapped wide awake again.

There was a silence. Then, "You know I can't, baby." Her voice was soft and regretful. "Just because we're in love is no excuse to ruin other people's lives."

"People in love should be married."

"Oh, honey." A folding chair moved. "You know Lily could never marry anyone in New Orleans if she had an African-American step-dad."

I raised my head, but I could only see kerosene light squaring tiny glittering sections of the screen.

"But this is adultery. It's a sin."

She sighed.

"And I've got to stop, Eva. Sneaking around. Hiding. Committing a sin, and still knowing I can't be with you all the time."

"I'll divorce Mason and we can live together if that's what you want, but I can't marry you. Not in New Orleans," she said gently.

"That's not enough. We'd still be in danger of going to hell."

"Oh, honey, there's no hell."

"You can't guarantee that."

There was a silence. Then Mrs. P. said so softly that I almost missed it, "No, I can't guarantee it."

She waited a second before she added, "If you could only break out of that damned Baptist shell that—"

"Don't blaspheme, Eva." But his voice was pleading not angry. "If we could just marry— I can't risk burning for eternity no matter how much I love you."

"I can't compromise Lily's chances. You know she isn't the prettiest or the brightest—" She broke off. "Oh, honey, I can't take away what little she has no matter how much I love you."

Someone got up to pace.

"If we can't get married, I don't see anything but to stop seeing each other."

The pacing stopped, and the kerosene spat a new brightness onto the screen.

"If that's the way you feel, baby, I can't take responsibility for sending you to your Baptist hell."

"Please, Eva. Please marry me."

"I can't."

The porch became so quiet I could hear mosquitoes whining to get in, and before Mrs. P. and Armond started talking again I must have dozed off, because when I opened my eyes, morning rain was streaking dirt and dead leaves down the window.

We drove back across the lake into rain that flew at us like horizontal strings of bee-bees. No one talked.

Not long after that, my mother's agency opened an office in Houston, and we moved there for her to sell fake Georgian mansions in River Oaks. Lily and I kept in touch the way kids do with scrawled Christmas cards and a once-in-a-while telephone call, but my senior year, my mom decided I could fly over for Mardi Gras.

I took a taxi from the airport and tabulated the changes six years and a couple of hurricanes had made on Airline and Carrollton. But when we got to Prytania, there was the Parrish house, exactly the same, the etched glass in the door and the dragonfly green trim looking just as it always had.

I rang the bell, and Mrs. Parrish came to the door appearing only a little older.

"Come in, honey. That was sweet of your mother to think of this. Lily's in a social club at school, but she'll be here at five. Come have a café-au-lait with me."

Somehow it didn't surprise me that Lily was in a social club.

"Mason's at some lawyer's convention in Washington, but he'll be back in time to take you girls to the Pontalba before the parades."

I followed her into the kitchen, half-expecting Armond to be sipping coffee at the table. But he wasn't, and despite the marbled gold stained glass in the windows, there was a strange lack of light in the room.

"I really came to have a cup of your café-au-lait anyway," I said. But I'd been rehearsing it, and the beat was wrong.

"Coming right up." She busied herself with the filter and French Market Coffee, whose red coffee can was the same, and I sat in the chair I'd always used. She talked about Lily and asked about my school, and then asked whether I thought Lily would like Tulane and I'd like Rice, until finally in a lull, I blurted, "How's Armond?"

It was as if she'd been waiting for me to ask.

"We talk on the phone sometimes. He and Denise did get a divorce, and she's in Chicago like she always wanted." She got out milk and the small saucepan that was the same enameled one of six years earlier. "He's a deacon in his church now, wouldn't you know."

I nodded, but she was staring down at the pan, her cheekbones in the sallow light scored and grayish under her skin. "I ran into him in a hardware store on Freret once."

She glanced at me but I knew she wasn't seeing me.

"That was four years, eight months, and ten days ago," she said.

A CHANGE IN THE WEATHER

The half moan, half scream, came from the back of the house, echoing down the hall from the room the newlyweds used as their bedroom, and the old woman in the kitchen listened to that second cry following hard upon the first.

She clamped her lips, the way she'd been firming them for the last month, ever since they'd moved in, and her jaw ridged before she forcibly relaxed her clenched teeth and said softly, "If I could only be certain what Mary Sam really wants."

She folded herself onto a kitchen chair and picked up one of the sneakers she'd placed beside the table the night before. "They was both just too young to get married. All their kinfolks should've seen that." Her thumb edged back and forth on the cushioned rim of the shoe as she stared down at the thick tread of the sole and the hot pink logo. It was a shame Schroeder's or the catalogue hadn't offered good working shoes like these when she herself had been young and just married. She could have helped Roy more and maybe they could have prospered.

She slipped the shoe on and worked the Velcro with bloated fingers.

"If only Roy hadn't up and died on me," she murmured while she fastened the sneakers and

---

stamped circulation back into her feet. Then she raised herself from the chair by placing her hands flat on the plastic cloth and leaning on the table. She went to the screen door whose mesh bulged loose from the wood molding. It would never have stayed gaped for more than an hour if Roy had been alive, but now she didn't focus on it as she stared out at the iron pipe fence marking the edge of her yard. A dry scrub oak sapling stood captive just inside the fence.

"Roy would've gazed off with them green eyes of his, would've mulled over for a day or two what should be done about Mary Sam and Laurence, and when he'd settled it in his head, he'd of laid it all out. And I'd know for sure it was the only thing to do."

Her glance strayed to the pasture beyond the rusting fence. The pasture land was no longer hers and no longer even a pasture, but merely a parched stretch of weeds as high as her waist, that had been bought by Art Freeley at the auction.

"Not that I begrudge Freeley the land," she repeated stubbornly in a fixed, rote litany. "It just rankles that he's got no more respect for good clover and buffalo grass than he has for that wore-out section of fesque he picked up from the Wilkins." She massaged her thumb, the wisest set of her bones. Thumbs always anticipated when a change of weather was due. "But then Art Freeley's only a kid, too, and who can tell what he's about any more than a body can know for sure what Mary Sam wants."

Boots sounded on the old hall boards, and Laurence came into the kitchen. "Well, there you are." He said it heartily as if she'd been gone. "Checking on Freeley's cattle this morning?"

"Thistle's no good for cattle," she said evenly, not turning to look at him. "And thistle's taken over out there."

"Yeah, we sure could use some rain," he agreed with the same heartiness as if she'd mentioned the heat.

He leaned slightly to peer at the cloudless blue of the sky, and she glanced sideways at him.

His tee-shirt was too tight, but needed another washing that would shrink it even more. His jeans settled low on his hips and let the knobs of fat balance on the rim of his tooled leather belt, hand-made by some girl he said had been crazy after him. His name, LAURENCE, was spelled out in fancy leather script, and he always laughed and said, "That's the way *I* spell it. With a U," whenever anyone remarked on it.

"Me and Mary Sam was wondering if you could use a couple of beers. It's damned hot," he said hopefully, still hunched over to study the sky, aligning himself with her granddaughter as if to remind her that she owed him the loyalty of a family member. "I'd be happy to go get us a six pack."

"A beer would be nice," she said. Nothing in her voice betrayed what she might be thinking, and her gaze remained steadily on his belt before she turned again to the should-be pasture.

"Mary Sam, I'm off," he called. "How about if I snag some chips, too?"

The question was addressed to her.

Since she'd often expressed a fondness for potato chips that had also come along too late in her life for her to get enough of them, she had to pull her eyes back from the thistle-choked land and look at him.

He might have been a good-looking kid except for his strange coloring. His skin gleamed cooked sunburn red from chin to cheekbones, maggot white from eyebrows to hairline, with the hollows around his eyes shadowed nearly blue. She'd often mentioned to Mary Sam that he should take to leaving off his ball cap so he could get something approaching an even tan. As it was, he resembled a wooden doll somebody'd painted in patriotic colors as a joke. Mary Sam always laughed, but she never passed on the suggestion.

He stood watching her and waiting for an answer, so finally she said, "Chips would be welcome."

"Chips and beers coming up." He bobbed a jerky grin, whipped his cap from its peg beside the gun rack, and jammed it on his head. JOHN DEERE in gold thread vibrated above the green bill. "Be right back."

He ducked past her and bounded down the back steps.

She watched as he flung himself into the pick-up and slammed the door. The motor started the instant the door shut, and she sighed. She had to offer him credit for that. He kept his truck in good shape, and the motor always took off the second he turned the key.

She stood without moving as an instant column of dust obscured the shimmering metallic blue cab and slow footsteps sounded in the hall.

She turned as her granddaughter came heavily into the kitchen.

The girl walked with the gait of the ninth month, and she blinked against the brilliant reflection of sunlight on the plastic tablecloth. The side of her face showed dark blotched red.

Mary Sam had always been such a happy little girl, never sitting still. Always leaping, jumping, laughing a deep-throated laugh that didn't belong to, or even seem to have come from, such a thin-chested child. She bounced, hopped, and hung from her knees like a spidery monkey on the pipe fence around the yard while she hollered, "Come see the world upside down, Grandma. Come see!"

"I like my world right side up, thank you," she'd say, and Mary Sam would laugh.

"Is he gone?" the girl asked.

Her cheek would be a yellow-blue bruise by morning.

"He's gone." Then she said without considering, withou mulling it over, "Mary Sam, honey, the world don't need to be this upside down."

The girl's great gold brown eyes, the color of good pumpkin pie, looked at her, and there might have been a spark glimmering in them.

"Now you do as I say, honey, and go lock the front door."

Mary Sam didn't protest, and she may have moved more quickly as she went back into the hall.

"And put the night chain on."

With the noon sun directly overhead and clouds as yet unformed for that cooling spell, the kitchen would be hot and airless the minute she shut the back door, and she took a deep breath.

But there was nothing for it now.

Even without Roy's help, she'd commenced it. And now she had to see it through.

She tugged the heavy door shut, kicking it with her sneaker to help it along. Laurence was fixing to shave it down so it wouldn't stick, but like everything else he said he'd tend to, he never got around to it. She hit the lock with her palm to make the metal tongue catch, and the blow jabbed pain through her hand.

She massaged it gently as she hooked her elbow through a chair back and dragged the chair to the door. She climbed on it awkwardly and reached for the shotgun in the gun rack Laurence was aiming to paint white one day soon.

Her fingers slid along the polished stock, and she looked at the gun with appreciation. She was a good shot and would have been a good hunter if she could have gone with Roy during deer season. But women joining in the hunt was something else that had come too late, and she sighed again.

She got off the chair, plucked two shells from the spice rack drawer where she kept them, and placed the brass and rose-colored columns in the barrel grooves. The pair fit sleek and gleaming, the brass buttons on the end proclaiming their maker in print too tiny for her eyes to decipher any longer.

Roy always said there was nothing prettier than a shell, any kind of shell, and during the war he'd welded the tree that sat on the parlor mantle from spent brass casings. She didn't use the parlor much these days, and she hadn't looked at the stylized tree since before Mary Sam and Laurence came.

She took another breath, sat down at the kitchen table and laid the shotgun across the plastic cloth to wait. Her puffed hand, resting on the plastic, began to sweat as a pick-up coming from the direction of Schroeder's turned into the dirt drive.

"You got everything shut up?" she called.

"Yes."

The truck skidded to a halt, the cab door opened, banged shut, and boots crunched over the yard as Mary Sam appeared in the kitchen doorway.

The screen door opened and the doorknob turned. The door panels wavered with his shove. The paper bag containing the six-pack and the chips crackled, and the door shuddered.

"Hey," Laurence called. "This damned door's stuck again. Somebody come pull from inside while I push."

"No." She raised her voice to carry through the door. "It's not stuck. It's locked."

A pause, a breath-held wait, expanded for a second before he repeated, "Hey!"

"I'll put your trash in a box and you can send somebody over to pick it up tomorrow."

A longer, startled silence hung in the air while the brown paper of the sack rattled again.

"Hey! What's going on?"

"You're not welcome here anymore," she said louder. "You can send someone, but don't you come back."

Mary Sam watched the door with no expression.

The door shook and the side hinges, held in place by years of white paint, quivered beneath their coated screws.

"Mary Sam's my wife."

"No," she said. "You didn't treat her like a wife should be treated, so I reckon you forfeited the husband role."

After another long, unbelieving silence, a great shove bowed the door panels. "I'm coming in there to get my wife."

"You don't have a wife here any longer." She moved the gun along the tabletop, crumpling up the cheap plastic, and cocked the safety off before she said anything else so he wouldn't miss the click. "I got the shotgun pointed right at you, son. I won't even have to open the door to blow you off them steps. Now you get in your truck and leave. Don't come back. Not ever, not for any reason, you hear?"

Silence. Then, "You can't just—"

"You get going by the time I count to three, or I'll pull the trigger." Her voice was as steady as the shotgun leveled at the door. She waited less than a second before she said, "One."

His boots landed on the gravel in one leap. "You old—"

"Two."

The pick-up door opened.

"You old . . . hag!"

But he was shouting from inside the cab.

"Three."

The truck door slammed and the motor accelerated before she got the syllable out. Tires spun front yard gravel against the iron fence and porch rails, pocked the wood on the front door with river pebbles as the truck sped away in the direction of town.

"You think he'll stay gone, Grandma?"

"Since he lost his bluster to a old lady like me, he won't show his face here again. I reckon he'll send Tolliver over to pick up his box."

It had been the right thing to do. But Roy wasn't there to tell her it was right, and a coil in the pit of her stomach twisted upward toward her ribcage. She didn't look again at Mary Sam, but kept gazing out on the clouds beginning to gather over the hot yellow pasture that was no longer good for running cattle and was no longer Roy's or hers.

TWENTY-SEVEN MINUTES TO MEMPHIS

She may not create an image of them every ninety seconds, but their rice-grain teeth, their irises—dark enough to shade the corneas blue—always lie near the rind of her consciousness. And as she fastens the seatbelt, she hears the echo of her childless sister, "Of course a prop plane is safe. If you're in such a hurry to get home to your twins—who are perfectly fine with Joel—you'll save three damned hours if you fly Air Link."

She didn't try to explain that Joel doesn't constantly hold them in his mind to enable their existence, that he can't prevent their sipping bleach, stepping off curbs into the paths of hurtling cars, or plunging baby fingers into disposal blades the way she can. She didn't say that no one else repeats the hourly incantations that keep them safe.

She glances at six seats along the aisle, but doesn't focus on them as she murmurs silently, Don't let anything happen to the twins.

The pilot says pleasantly over his shoulder, "All right, ladies and gentlemen, we're taking off now." He smiles and buffs his sandy crew-cut. "It's a twenty-seven minute flight to Memphis."

He nods toward emergency directions on the door, recites cautions about not smoking, about not disabling the smoke detector in the lavatory, about not using electronic devices during take-off. "Make sure your seatbelts are securely fastened." He swerves his attention to the controls, fingering levers and knobs as if he's driving a limousine.

The propellers spin, and he peers out one window, then the other as he taxis down the runway. The propellers become silver discs, and the plane gathers speed.

No discernible difference marks the race down the runway and the lift-off, and the only indication of flight is that treetops slide below the wings and the red needle of the altimeter circles steadily.

She sits directly behind the pilot and watches the dials illuminated in electric green. The digital dashboard clock reads 3:22.

Don't let anything happen to them, she says without moving her lips. She leans back and looks out the window as they surge through a prickling white mist to skim the crust of clouds.

But abruptly the white billows shade to gunmetal gray, and heavy drops snake across the double window panes. The pilot switches on windshield wipers so like those of a car that she has to smile.

Lightning flashes, imprinting a zig-zag of blue-yellow on the unexpectedly grime-black clouds. Rain pelts the metal plane skin, thickens as if the plane has swooped under a waterfall. Another flare sparks and thunder drowns the sound of the motor.

Suddenly the plane drops, and the seat falls away. She jolts into the cushion as the plane thuds to the floor of the air pocket. Her viscera accordions, sends nerve jabs through her thighs. Before she adjusts to the jar, the plane throbs upward, then drops again. The red altimeter needle whirls.

The plane bucks, and someone across the aisle says, "Christ."

She doesn't look at the speaker, but glances at the seat beside the pilot and realizes there's no co-pilot.

The overhead lights blink on. Rain clouds entomb the sky into midnight black despite the fact that the digital clock says 3:31.

Bolts of lightning cut the blackness with the regularity of flashing neon, dancing closer to the silver wings.

What happens if lightning strikes a plane? she asks silently. Are the occupants electrocuted? Will the aircraft sling-shot into the nearest mountain with a cargo of charred bodies?

The plane plummets again.

Will the next drop, or the one after that, crack the little plane apart, drop it in careless halves over a stand of cedars?

She studies the clock and calculates. Fourteen minutes to the Memphis airport.

We have to stay in the air only fourteen minutes more, she repeats silently. Then she adds inadvertently, Don't let us crash.

The shock is that no other litany echoes in her head. If the plane smashes into a stone outcropping, and purses, books and severed arms, fragments of aluminum and shreds of luggage arch into the brush, Joel will have to manage without her. When he wakes at two a.m. and asks if everything will be all right, he'll have to find someone else to reassure him. He'll have to keep reading *Good-night, Moon* at bedtime, and he'll have to approve whatever hop-scotch squares the twins draw on their sunny sidewalk, whatever mica stones they find on the two-block walk to school. She's never mentioned she uses Bavarian sauerkraut on the Reuben sandwiches they like, or that the recipe for her carrot cake is a newspaper clipping. There's too much she hasn't mentioned. But they'll have to get along alone if she spins to earth and rainwater thins the mangled tissue in her crushed skull.

Does everyone about to die realize—as easily and quickly as she's conceded it—that the rest of the world will have to go on without them? Is that how suicides think? She asks the face reflected in the mirror window. Even suicidal mothers? Encapsulated in crystal cocoons of self, is that what they accept as they step into the weight of a noose or warm a pistol barrel on their tongues?

The aisle lights black out as the plane plunges.

It hangs briefly, drops again, and she tenses, her hands so tight against the armrests that the rough weave lances her palms.

But she reminds herself that sleeping children and relaxed drunks have a better chance to survive, and she forces her fists limp, forces her breath steady.

The control panel still works, and the plane is flying nearly horizontal.

A blast of thunder rolls, quiets, and the sound of the motor surfaces. If they can stay up for eleven more minutes, they'll survive.

She rivets her attention on the squares of revolving numbers, tries to ignore the lurching, the lightning and rain. Four, five. But then the minute square holds the next luminous number motionless, and it's as if time stops.

A slash of lightning remains suspended so long, so brilliantly, that she shuts her eyes against it. Green residual specks spray the inner sides of her eyelids. The plane careens sideways, and the air spout blows air on her nostrils, unaccountably hot and cheerful.

The plane rights itself, and she opens her eyes just as the pilot glances ashen-faced out the window.

But the minute slots of the clock have moved. Only seven minutes more.

If the storm hasn't delayed them.

That phrase wrenches her stomach without a movement from the plane.

She's been watching the clock, relying on the numbers to time them down alive, but what if the clock is already meaningless? What if they've been struck by a brilliant lightning bolt and are already dead? What if they're already a planeload of wraiths flying into the eternity of seven eternal minutes?

She stares out at the rain. The interior lights abruptly return, and she's reflected again in the black window.

Seven infinite minutes. Thunder rumbles, and the aircraft labors against the rain. She closes her eyes, but no images appear in the emptiness of the endless flight, and she waits as the plane hangs in the dark void.

They lunge downward. She automatically clutches the tweed armrest.

But when she opens her eyes, the minute square of the clock has changed. If they, by some fluke of luck are still on schedule, they need only five more minutes to land safely.

Thunder crashes, a wall of water hits the plane, and the metal shudders.

But the clock numbers ease forward, independent of the tidal storm, of the lives linked to their almost imperceptible movement.

3:45. Only four more minutes.

Then three.

The plane dips with unexpected violence, but as she releases her startled intake of breath, she looks at the pilot. His white knuckled hands are turning the wheel.

He must be aiming toward an airport.

A crash landing won't be like a rock catapulted through the clouds to fall with the acceleration of mass multiplied by gravity. If the pilot, not the storm, maintains control, they can ease to earth. The Memphis airport must sit on a level stretch beyond high-rises, suburban density, and the river. If they get close, they'll have a chance.

She watches the scarlet needle. They're nosing down through the unchanging black rain. The clock says they're a minute away.

How near can they be to avoid being blown apart on impact? Can forty or thirty seconds set them down alive?

Then a blue light shows through the windshield and the gloom. It has to be a ground light, and she stares intently ahead, absorbed in the spot of illumination, pulling against the seatbelt that keeps her from rising.

The light separates into a series of blue points, into the dots of a runway border. And she concentrates with the pilot on centering the wheels between mercury blue lines, on speeding down the wet tarmac until the tires touch. She locks breath in her lungs until the lighted windows of the tower glimmer through the dark afternoon.

They brake with a quivering drag.

By six o'clock, the rain abates, and she waits with refreshed mascara for her connecting flight. But as she stands by the ticket counter, a scene unfurls of Joel sideswiped, of the children bleeding in their car seats, and as she seems to gaze calmly through the plate glass, she blinks the ritual, Don't let anything happen to them.

THE SETTLEMENT

Dale Barnes aligned his raw-silk burgundy tie with such a deliberate, subtle gesture that only someone watching closely would notice his attention had strayed from his companion in the hotel bar.

His companion and client, the gray-haired CEO of a Catholic-school uniform company and New Orleans' Father of the year, sat watching him—not closely—and repeated for the third time, "Janine Dawson never set foot in my beach house." He sipped a scotch while his gray eyes gazed across the marble-topped table at Dale. "My wife is having the place redone, and it'd be lunacy to bring some woman in for romance with the champagne glasses still in boxes."

"She described the house to Miss Longchamps." Dale Barnes had perfected a subtle non-confrontational style, and his words held no hint of contradiction.

The silver eyes widened. "God, Barnes, do you suppose she went down there and looked in the windows?"

"It's possible."

"No one in his right mind would suggest an affair on a mattress on the floor."

"Where are the bedrooms?"

"On the second floor."

"Then if she looked in the window, she wouldn't see the sleeping arrangements."

He patted the client's sleeve. "I wouldn't worry about it."

"Thank God Nathan sent you."

Dale merely smiled, and as soon as he left the bar, he went to his suite and called his senior partner. "We could have handled this one by U.S. mail, Nathan."

Nathan laughed. "I said I'd send my pit-bull best. When does the girl show?"

"Nine tomorrow. I don't think she's got a damned thing going for this suit but nuisance value, so I figure on an early lunch at Arnaud's."

"Well, I sent you over to settle cheap. Save their company enough to have a good bottle of wine with lunch."

The following morning, as the bells of St. Louis Cathedral clanged nine, Dale Barnes conveyed a sheaf of depositions from his briefcase to the polished Queen Anne table and sat down in a wingchair to wait.

In the echo of inhaled silence after the ninth chime, the wheel-creak of a carriage reached the suite.

The night before as he got out of his taxi at the hotel, Dale had encountered such a horse-drawn carriage, and he'd stood at the curb while the driver, in stovepipe hat and frockcoat, white-gloved a woman into the passenger seat, mounted the driver's box with the aplomb of an ante-bellum coachman, and clopped the horse off down the street.

Now he listened to the horseshoes on ancient brick as he put his palm on the receiver of one of the suite phones, this one forest green to match the velvet upholstery. He practiced a first impression of impatience, of business more urgent than any plaintiff's accusation, and when the knock came, he lifted the receiver. "The door's open."

A girl, anywhere from twenty to thirty-five—he'd never been good at judging the ages of women—clicked across the foyer toward the carpet.

No one had mentioned that Janine Dawson was black.

And as Dale motioned at the wingchair opposite his, it became abruptly clear why Nathan had sent the firm's newest partner.

Janine Dawson folded herself onto the green velvet chair with her spine rigid.

"All right, let me know as soon as you confirm," he said to the dial tone before he hung up and sat studying the girl. "I understand you already told your story to Miss Longchamps, but I want you to tell it to me."

"Where do you want me to start?" She looked at him steadily, her lashes curling into the chocolate petal smoothness of her eyelids.

Five years earlier he might have marveled at the cool assurance of her shakedown, but now, too far from the bar exam for that, he said in an objective tone, "You had your job for eight months?"

"Eight months and three weeks."

He uncapped the gold pen with which his wife had rewarded the partnership and took up a yellow pad. "You said you were promised a raise, and you told Miss Longchamps you went to Mr. Copeland's office to make sure you were getting it."

"I expected it to be more or less automatic."

"Did you?" He wrote that down even though her expectation already appeared in the typed copy on the table.

"But Mr. Copeland said he'd been working on the employee reviews at his beach house and that he'd left them there." She'd obviously well rehearsed her story. "He said he needed to have them in by closing, so he suggested we run over and pick them up."

"You didn't see anything out of the ordinary in that suggestion?" He used the irony with which he'd demolished enough witnesses to make partner.

She didn't seem to notice. "Lyla Meadows was up for a raise, too, and Mr. Copeland said he felt foolish not remembering to bring everything back from the beach. But with workmen and all, he said he simply forgot."

"So you agreed to drive to the beach in the middle of the day?"

She either missed or ignored that implication as well. "I didn't really need to go back to my desk, so I said I'd be up for a drive. It was worth it to get our raises."

He waited a glacial moment before he prompted, "And—"

"On the drive, he talked business and asked my opinion about the new line of jumpers." The curling lashes blinked. "I thought he was being a good boss, getting to know me, wanting my input."

He studied her a moment. "I can see you'd be a formidable witness on the stand."

"What?"

"Nothing. Go on."

"It wasn't until we got to the beach house that he changed." She paused, began again. "When we went in through the sliding door, he got out a bottle of wine."

"You didn't begin to suspect he might have more than business on his mind?"

"He said I deserved a drink for being such a good sport going to the Gulf and all."

"I see."

"But it was as if—"

He waited, and for the first time she glanced down at the verdant nap of velvet.

"After one glass of wine, he started grabbing me and using words like—"

Fourteen years earlier, fresh from Alice, Texas, in his freshman year of college, Dale Barnes had gone with his roommate to a small Austin club. The singer at the piano had been dark and thin and beautiful, and his roommate had grabbed for her, had used language no one in Alice used. And now, Dale sat looking at Janine Dawson a moment too long in the brilliant hotel sunlight before he said, "Can you describe the house?"

"Of course I can. Do you want me to?"

He cleared his throat. "Before we can address your complaint, we have to know you were there."

"Mr. Copeland says I wasn't?"

"My firm *is* representing his company."

"So you can't tell me what he said," she agreed without animosity. "Well, I was there. And he tried to—"

He waited and focused on the legal pad. He held the pen loosely in his square fingers. "Just describe the house."

She took a breath. "He'd been telling the truth about having work done. Drop cloths covered the floors, paint buckets were everywhere." She began a description that included wallpaper patterns, shades of enamels on baseboards, the metallic composition of light fixtures and chandeliers, and the shapes of the mantelpiece stones.

"That's all visible from outside, you know. You didn't have to go inside."

"But I did go inside. Through the sliding door of the family room." She looked at him solemnly. "Do you want me to continue?"

He nodded.

She described the black fixtures of one bathroom, the blue of the other, the slate on the kitchen floor, the brushed-nickel appliances, the shelving in the den. "Since everything was in boxes, he got glasses from a carton. There wasn't a thing in the refrigerator but two bottles of wine and a corkscrew. I thought *that* was funny, but I guess if you drink wine with corks, it's dumb not to have a corkscrew handy."

He nodded again.

"I knew it was expensive wine, but the paint smelled so strong, I couldn't taste it."

His wife always said women noticed more objects, more colors, more smells, more of everything than men, and he'd stopped jotting notes by the time Janine Dawson added, "What was so ridiculous was that there was no furniture, not even on the second floor which Mr. Copeland said had the best view of the Gulf. When he made his move, he tried to pull me down onto a bare mattress. I shoved him away and told him he was crazy."

After a long pause, he said, "What did he do then?"

"He grabbed me again, and if he hadn't been drunk by that time—" She glanced at the velvet arm of the chair again. "But he said things that—"

After an even longer pause he said softly, "I suppose you've thought about what would be fair compensation for your— for your unhappy experience."

"I can't work there any more," she said. "He might not remember what he said, but I do, and I can't be around him. It was a job I really liked. I was good at it. He was just elected Father of the Year, too. Isn't that crazy?"

The gold pen hung poised for bargaining. "So what do you think would be fair?"

Her obsidian eyes gazed at him. "I thought six months pay might—"

He didn't move. "Six months pay?" The pen point tipped the yellow page. "Maybe you don't know that—"

"I wouldn't ask for it with the raise," she amended quickly.

"I don't think you realize—"He broke off and sat pensive, not looking at her while the cathedral bell chimed a number he didn't count.

Then he got up and went toward the bedroom. The carpet muffled his step.

At the door he looked back. "You thought it over carefully. Six months pay?"

She nodded.

When he closed the bedroom door, he stood with his back against if for a moment before he crossed to the phone and dialed Houston.

"She wants six months pay," he said without preamble when Nathan answered.

"She wants what?"

"Six months pay."

"Jesus. They'd cough up half a million to settle this one."

"Half a million? They'd go that high?"

"Doesn't she know the checkbook's open?" Nathan asked.

After a pause, Dale Barnes said, "No, she doesn't."

"God damn, buddy, you are the best. I knew I was right to send you. A first time out and you get six months fucking pay!" When the pause lengthened, he added, "Most women don't have a clue what they're worth, do they? Is she a looker?"

Dale Barnes didn't answer either question. "What shall I tell her?"

"Hell, buddy, tell her we agree."

He laid the receiver into its molded cradle and took three, then four, breaths.

In the street below, an antebellum carriage pulled up to the lobby door, and outside the window, a woman tourist giggled. A man's laugh spiraled up to the suite as Dale Barnes straightened the wine-colored tie that didn't need straightening and started back across the deep carpet toward the room where the beautiful, dark and slender girl sat waiting.

WAKEFIELD O'CONNOR

He was a dwarf.

There was no viable euphemism once you realized his total height was four-foot nine and that foreshortened arms, legs, and neck attached to the large handsome head and the heavy-boned hands and feet. His size and awkward gait would have made him recognizable in any school, but, of course, in our little school in our little Gulf town we never had to articulate the word "dwarf" since everyone in every class knew Wake already.

He was the first real politician any of us had ever encountered, and if someone new transferred in, you only had to say, "You know, Wake O'Connor, the sophomore (or later the junior and then the senior) class president." He'd mastered all four hundred and six names in the school, and he didn't hesitate to yell down the row of lockers, "Hey, Courtney," if he wanted a favor. To be as openly, and joyfully, manipulative as he was, anyone would have to be smart, but Wake was actually nudging brilliant. I used to watch him work the crowd at school assemblies, and I always marveled at how he utilized his truncated stature and his really startling smile to charm.

Wake, Neely Prescott, and I rode the same bus to Pasadena High, and since our dads all worked for

Standard Oil, we hung out together, studied chemistry together, and got into Rice University together.

I'd thought Wake's intelligence might have shone brighter in our high school than it would at Rice, but he glittered among all the other valedictorians and salutatorians as radiantly as he had in Pasadena's trig class. He was also just as political, and after the first semester, I could see he'd easily be president of our college class.

"Wake is phenomenal," I said to Neely.

"Of course he is." And as usual when she heard his name, she blushed.

I admired Wake, but Neely adored him, and I often wanted to shake her, to tell her not to stare at him with such worship. But I couldn't think how to say it or how to warn her that she'd probably never be more than a buddy to him, so I kept telling myself that someday his sensitivity and the understanding born of his own distinction would allow him to appreciate Neely. But I also knew that in our generation, it was hard for a male of any size not to desire the starlet types featured in *Playboy*.

And because her face had smashed against the dashboard in the same car wreck that had killed her mother, Neely had stopped being pretty at ten-years-old despite her luxuriant platinum hair and slim model's figure. In fact, having such beautiful hair and such a gorgeous body undoubtedly only accentuated the shock when she turned around with her crushed lips and mangled nostrils which no amount of surgical repair had been able to modify into a less equine face.

I spent a lot of time arranging double dates for her via whichever engineer or chemist I was going out with, but only once in a while could I convince Wake to include her in our group that was wearing sea-urchin drapery for an Archi-Arts ball or in a crowd gathering for a cook-out on Galveston beach.

Strangely enough, however, when it came time for our senior prom, he didn't have a date, and I persuaded him to ask Neely.

She floated into my apartment to tell me.

And two weeks before the prom, she laid out her scarlet lace dress and dyed-to-match pumps on my couch, where she planned to spend the night after the dance.

I'd agreed to go with Ron, who drove us all in the conservative Chrysler his father gave him for graduation.

I remember the prom itself as a typical spring dance with summer tuxedos, strapless gowns, and linen pumps that became increasingly begrimed as each girl's escort became increasingly lubricated. But both Ron and Wake stayed relatively sober throughout the dancing, the midnight bar-be-cue, and the drive back to my place.

"If you've got an extra hunk of floor, I'd like to talk you out of it for tonight," Wake said to me as we piled from Ron's car. "I need to go to Austin tomorrow, and I'd as soon take off from here."

"It's all right with me if Neely doesn't mind. The only extra floor is in the living room."

"Oh, I don't mind." Even in starlight, her blush became visible.

They strolled inside to give Ron and me a chance to neck on the steps, but since Ron's single talent was that he could dance, we stood for only a few minutes before we said goodnight and he drove off.

The apartment was dark, but I could see the merged shadow of Wake and Neely entwined on the couch, and I tip-toed by and shut the bedroom door before I snapped on the light.

Wake had draped his rented tux jacket on the desk chair, and it gleamed white and broad shouldered beside the night table.

I didn't notice what time it was then or later when he came into the bedroom and stumbled against the chair. "Sorry," he whispered. "I was afraid I'd left my wallet in Ron's car."

It was a more feeble excuse than I'd have expected from him as I watched him carry the wallet into the living room and shut the door. But I thought that since he'd remembered to bring a condom, maybe Neely was in the running after all.

When I came out the next morning, I knew immediately she'd had no chance whatsoever.

Wake was making coffee in the tiny kitchenette. "If I could have found a skillet, I'd have scrambled us some eggs," he said.

Neely appeared in the archway in my bathrobe. She gazed at him, her brown eyes enormous with adoration.

He didn't acknowledge her.

"I use a saucepan to scramble eggs," I said shortly. "Neely, you get the cups."

It was almost impossible not to lunge into each other in the confined space, but Wake managed to avoid even brief contact with her while he broke eggs into the pan and folded the whites and yolks together.

By the time we carried plates of egg and toast to the living room, I could tell he wasn't going to look at her or speak to her.

You son-of-a-bitch, I thought. It's all right for you to screw, but any female who lets you screw her is a slut.

But I didn't know how to snarl at him without flaying Neely, and I had to sit and nod and pretend I didn't notice he was ignoring her, pretend I didn't know why.

A week later we graduated, scattered, and I lost touch with Neely.

Wake and I moved on to law schools, and while I focused on Louisiana's Napoleonic Code, he stayed in Dallas at SMU. But I occasionally heard about him, and I knew that around the time I ran into Ted, Wake married someone named Carla.

Our tenth college reunion came and went, then the fifteenth and twentieth before I read in the alumni magazine that Neely had died somewhere in Africa. I debated about contacting her father, but I didn't, just as I didn't attend our twenty-fifth class reunion. And it wasn't until the thirtieth that I went back to Rice.

Naturally, I recognized Wake from across the room.

His black hair had turned curly gray, but his blue eyes glittered the same intense sapphire, and his assured grin flashed the same dimple as ever.

"I hoped you'd be here." He grabbed me into a muscle-bruising hug. "Did you bring a spouse?"

"Ted's a New Yorker. He'd rather be boiled in a vat of Chivas Regal than go to a Texas college reunion. Did you bring yours?"

"Our daughter-in-law's ready to deliver, so Carla stayed home. We've been to these before when you didn't show."

"Is this one significantly different?"

He laughed. "At the others, we thought we still had things to achieve, but now we realize we're just going to keep making money."

A waiter passed with a tray of champagne, and Wake lifted off two glasses.

"Did you hear about Neely?" I asked as I accepted one.

He nodded. "She was in Kenya, helping natives build industries not based on elephant ivory. They never caught the hunters who shot her."

We sipped the champagne.

"How come we didn't keep up with each other?" he said then. "We're even in the same profession."

I looked down at him. "It was probably the senior prom."

"The prom?"

I nodded. "You screwed Neely on my couch."

"I did?"

"You don't even remember?"

He considered. "And you held that against me?"

"Not that. But the next morning you treated her with complete contempt."

I put the glass down and watched the bubbles gyrate in the stem. "I guess I always thought you'd escaped that damned Texan, virgin/whore view of women. I always thought you were different from the others."

He studied me a moment before he shook his head.

"You and Neely were always such innocents, such idealists." His big hand patted mine. "I was never different from anyone else. I was just shorter."

ARRIVING ON THE 7:10

Despite his assurances that nothing will keep him from seizing her in his arms the moment her foot—"Wear those sexy shoes with the gold buckles"—touches the platform, he isn't there.

The other passengers bound from nubbed metal train stairs, stride across the concrete slab and down the concrete steps. They shelter briefcases in the misting rain as they duck from the station's eaves, and to catch anyone's attention, she'd have to grab a raincoated arm and raise her voice over the dripping water. But he's reminded her to expect no Southern courtesy from commuters who shun eye contact, and who, he says, jog past someone prone on the tarmac without a pitying glance. "You'll have to shelve those Southern belle wiles," he said while he laughed affectionately and stroked her hair.

The platform clears, and if she inadvertently hoped he'd be shadowed in his Mercedes, discretely avoiding the streetlight and neighbors who might know his wife, that hope fades when the last rain-slick car pulls away from the lot.

She shivers in the expensive black silk stole shot with eighteen karat threads and clicks toward the waiting room. She's paired the gold-buckled pumps to a classic black sheath under his Christmas shawl, and to create an initial impression of elegance, she snapped everything but her fashionable shoulder bag into an airport locker.

A wall clock shies buttery light toward the lobby window, and she calculates that the train pulled in and disappeared fourteen minutes earlier. He's clearly late.

She grasps the doorknob and pulls.

The door doesn't budge.

She tugs in surprise, then pushes with equal force. The door remains immobile.

She stares through the indifferently polished glass into a room tallow-hazed, empty, and she furiously rattles the door before she stops and glances at the vacant tracks.

Nothing stirs, and the only sound is the drip of collected vapor from the roof. But night is molding inscrutable black shadows into the corners, and she moves quickly to the edge of the platform.

A few minutes earlier she searched only for his car, but now she analyzes the nocturnal warehouses huddled darkly beyond the parking lot, the street—a gleam of wet pavement does sweep beside the station with its one streetlight—and the brushy silhouettes of trees flattened against night sky.

A pay phone balances on a pole at the foot of the stairs, and she studies it as she fumbles through the shoulder bag.

The plane was late, and she hurried from the airport to the train, assuming she'd charge her cell at his house, and although she's prudently brought his address and phone number, she didn't anticipate using either. So her fingers in the recess of the bag encounter only scattered change among the twenty-dollar bills, the negligee, and one plastic rectangle of her driver's license.

Oh, shit, she murmurs silently.

She takes a two-part breath and guides her suede pumps down the water-glazed concrete. Shit, shit, shit, she murmurs as each brass buckle descends each wet step.

Fine spume frosts her hair and the black/gold stole, and the phone hood is futile before she reaches it.

She came with no intention of calling his house, but since his wife, whom he so rarely mentions that it's as if there's no Angelica Leland after all, has been aboard her Carnival cruise for six days, and although he is undoubtedly, at this very moment, accelerating down his dangerous hill, she deposits her quarters. The metallic clang does produce a dial tone, and after she punches in the numerals on her scrap of paper, the comforting electricity of a ring pulses across the line.

After the fourth vibration, a woman's voice says, "You have reached the Leland residence. We're unable to come to the phone right now, but if you leave a message, we'll get back to you as soon as we can."

Of course she won't leave a message, and she stabilizes the receiver against the eddy of Angelica's "we" before she silences the phone.

As water gusts under the tin-scoop phone cover, her fingers dip for more coins to wedge into the slot, and she presses the O.

When a disinterested voice at last asks, "How can I help you?" she reels off quickly, "I need a cab to pick me up at—" She reads the station name from the wall. "I've used up my change, my cell phone is dead, and in case this phone doesn't give any change back from an operator call, could you please ring the nearest taxi company?"

A shocked silence ensues as if no one has ever made such a request, but finally the voice says, "I guess the nearest company would be the Gold Diamond Line."

"Thank you."

After another hesitation of sluiced rain and no discernible reverberation along the line, a man growls, "Gold Diamond."

"I need at taxi." She repeats the station name.

This time the stunned hiatus lengthens until she begins again, "I'm at—"

"That's twenty minutes from here, lady."

"I was told y'all were the closest cab line."

"Well, yeah."

"My ride didn't show up, and I need a taxi."

The man is silent. Then, "I'll have to charge you even if your ride shows up before my cab gets there."

"Of course."

"You'll stay there?"

Her confidence that a cab is being dispatched allows her to say, "I'll wait here even *after* my ride shows up."

"All right." It's a dubious acceptances, and he adds, "But like I say, it'll be at least twenty minutes."

Emanating an odor of wet wool and silk, she climbs the stairs again to stand on the platform and watch the streetlamp and the long intervals of blackness between sets of headlights that flare momentarily through the Chablis rain.

"Now I know what y'all mean about your lives up here not being black and white," she'll tell him. "It's black and yellow." And he'll throw back his head and laugh.

But what if he's lying comatose below Angelica's recorded request for messages?

What if he's had a heart attack? Or has tripped and fallen down his spiral staircase?

Headlights, raising panels of water like illuminated topaz glass, dazzle her before they extinguish themselves at the curve of the street.

What if he's hydroplaned the Mercedes on his raw hill and his beautiful graying temple is even now bleeding into an armrest?

A car with a pair of washed and brilliant lights sweeps into the station lot.

Since no yellow-lit crest indicates that it's a taxi, a vein in her forehead throbs.

Before she can croak his name, however, a voice calls from the citrine blind of water. "You the lady that ordered a cab?"

The steps are more treacherous in the stabbing glare, but she maneuvers them and splashes to the car, climbs into the back seat. "I didn't see your taxi light, but I need you to take me to this street." She proffers the address.

"Bulb's burned out." He peers at the paper and cocks his chin. "Up a hill. In some woods?"

"I think so."

"Your ride didn't show, eh?" He notches up the heater. "Where you from in the South?"

"Is it that obvious?"

"I been hauling fares a long time. I got a good ear." He crinkles at her from the rearview mirror, but he doesn't re-ask as they ascend, following the blacktop's double yellow lines toward a stand of trees.

She stares hard for a Mercedes, ditched or whizzing past to meet the 7:10. But the incline contains only a few lemony streetlamps, fewer yellow-lit window squares, and no cars.

"What's that number again?"

She reads it from the dash light.

"This is it then." He turns into a driveway, and a three-story Doric-columned house looms beyond the brooding hedge. As the taxi brakes, the headlight beam slams against the doors of a four-car garage. The house is dark except for a nimbus of lemony light deep in the black interior. "Looks like your friends ain't home."

"Maybe there's a note on the door." She slides out and dashes to the porch.

There's no note.

But the tiny lamp, in what is obviously a study, gleams with saffron intent on polished floors, a barrister bookcase, the upholstered arm of a wing chair. No body lies on the Oriental hall runner.

She steps off the porch again, and her heels purl through the wet gravel to the back door.

No note—or sign of an emergency exit—permeates the blackness.

She shields her make-up as she goes to the cab, grabs the shoulder bag from the back seat, and folds two twenties toward the driver. "I'm sure he'll—they'll— be back

He accepts the bills without looking. "What if they ain't?"

"I thought he might have had an accident, but..."

"She's going on 7:10. I'll wait here."

Speaking cheerfully now. "He knew I was arriving."

The driver is a voice beyond a curtain of yellow rain. "Okay. If you say so."

She returns to the porch as he backs out, glittering the length of hedge into focus. Light swings across the fat columns, across an abrupt yellowing oak in the yard before it vanishes, and night boxes her in impenetrable blackness.

She sinks onto a bench and wraps his stole around her. But rain has mulched it into a tangle of gold and silken filaments, and it's as if she's trying to bury herself in wet leaves.

Anything could have happened. He could have—

Invisible droplets blow onto the porch, and she flinches before she adds in a soft whisper, "But if he couldn't let me know earlier, he could have left word on the machine." She stands up. "He seems to have thought of everything else."

She peers through the half circle of glass at the shrouded hallway and jiggles the locked door before she sits again, shivers, and unfurls the stole from her shoulders.

Men simply have no idea.

She lays the stole on the bench.

Of course she can take care of herself, but—

She trusted him so completely.

How could he—how could all men—be so unaware?

She exhales a fractured breath. The blood in her sheer-stockinged feet has thickened with the cold.

I'm more alone, more vulnerable than I've ever been in my life, she says inside her head.

The wealthy Lelands have surely installed an alarm system. Maybe it's time to break in. When the police arrive, I'll explain.

A textural change interlaces the darkness, and the rain slacks into fog.

She closes her eyes.

What time is it now?

How much longer do I give him before I grope for a two-handed rock and smash the beveled glass in his front door?

The 7:10 arrived almost too long ago for memory.

Fog tendrils surround her face. Her all-day mascara has chilled to custard.

She wills her lashes immobile against her cheeks, inhales the blackness, slowly exhales invisible steam.

Perhaps it's already midnight.

Perhaps it's time to shatter the glass.

She breathes in steady concentration and tries to control her shiver.

Then an abrupt slash of light glares on her lids, jabs into her retina when her eyes jerk open.

Tires crunch up the drive.

The voice of the taxi driver says from behind the headlights, "I got to thinking."

She wobbles erect. "Did you?"

"It's kind of isolated for a lady to be up here alone. I'll take you to a hotel."

"Thank you."

She staggers off the porch and crosses the crushed rock. She opens the car door and doesn't glance back at the bench or at the dark mesh of the stole, which in the morning sunlight will glitter with hard metallic strands.

MADE IN THE U.S.A.

"Fran got her hundred percent on collars and they moved her to buttonholes this morning." The older woman with puckered eyelids pours sugar from the glass container into a Styrofoam cup. Her upper lip flattens against her teeth, morose but somehow smug, as she watches the coffee level inch toward the rim of the cup. "They do it every time."

The young woman at the end of the table glances at the speaker, at the other women fingering their own cups of weak coffee, also laced heavily with sugar, the only items in the factory besides toilet paper supplied by the company. Each woman has initialed the white Styrofoam with a red marker since the company issues only one fresh disposable cup every morning.

The young woman hasn't met anyone in the factory named Fran, and she has trouble following the older woman's monologue. For some reason the painted cinder block walls remind her of a barn, and her mind keeps straying to Toby, peering through his shed slats until she comes to let him out.

"—and nobody ever gets better than sixty percent on buttonholes. One of these days, those assholes will use our sorry percentages to outsource the whole she-bang." The woman's neck sways a loose curtain of flesh as she swigs her coffee.

The young woman pulls her thoughts away from Toby, tries to concentrate.

And when the buzzer sounds in the break room, she follows the others along the rows, around the carts and the women still at their machines whose ten minute break won't come for another half hour.

She adjusts herself behind the sewing machine surrounded by stacks of sleeves and stacks of jacket fronts and backs connected at the shoulder seams. She determinedly focuses on the routine. Spread and flatten the material, match the sleeve to the back and front armhole, sew around the curve, snip the thread. Fit another sleeve to the opposite armhole, center at the seam and stitch. Snip. Toss the jacket onto the cart behind her stool. Grab the next sleeve, center the outer edges of jean material together. Sew.

When she can finish both sleeves and toss the jacket over her shoulder in four minutes, twelve jackets sleeved in forty-eight minutes, she'll reach the hundred percent quota the factory requires.

Now, only the sleeves of the first jacket in the morning or the first after her lunch break go together in four minutes. The others take longer, and in the forty-eight minute sweep of the red hand on the clock attached to the tan wall, only ten jacket sets have been scooped from the piles, sewn, snipped, and flung over her shoulder. Only eighty-three percent according to the company's calculations. And that's if she doesn't go to the ladies' through the door beneath the clock, all the way at the end of the great room. As the checker explained, no one punches out unless it's quitting time or lunch time, and bathroom trips are subtracted from the forty-eight minutes.

Some of the girls say they feel an almost overwhelming urge to fold a jacket right side out and look at it, just to know the stitch has caught, that the seam is straight and worthy of a completed jacket, something they'd buy themselves if they picked it up in Walmart. But there's no time to turn the stiff jean material or examine the seam. The checker told her that some girls get good enough to make a hundred-and-ten or even a hundred-and-fifty percent. Perhaps if she gets that practiced, one-hundred-and-fifty-percent, then she can take a quick peek at her finished work.

Not yet though.

Grab a sleeve, match it firmly, clamp the machine foot over the jean stuff. Guide the electric needle around, release, snip.

Toby's narrow face surfaces on the jean material, his velvet eye framed by the boards of his stall as he watches for her.

Position the cut edges, dark jean blue facing dark blue, drop the metal foot.

Toby vanishes.

She avoids a glance at the whirling crimson minute hand.

Her arms have been scraped raw by the raveling jean cloth before she clocks out, and as she steps into the stiffened afternoon sunlight, she eases the itch by rubbing her wrists down her tee-shirt.

The vinyl seat of the pick-up is blistering, but fortunately her thighs are sheathed in the same heavy material she's been sewing and she can slide into the cab without wincing.

When she began sewing the sleeves in place, she occasionally imagined a completed jacket worn by a laughing girl with long tawny hair swirling in slow motion, her tapered, polished fingers flickering from the jean cuffs. But those images don't occur any longer, and it's as if the jacket sleeves are attached solely for the purpose of throwing them onto the cart.

The pick-up coughs, the rebuilt motor finally catches, and she steers the truck through the parking lot. The other women in her shift never seem in any hurry to leave the air-conditioned building, and perhaps she wouldn't rush out either if Toby weren't standing in the tin-roofed shed and if CW could raise his rented hospital bed without help. And today she has to stop for soda crackers and another six-pack of Pepsis on her way home.

The doctor is certain CW has had a mild stroke. "Unusual in someone as young as he is, but it happens."

While he talks, the pink-faced doctor alternately taps the desktop and the rim of his glasses with a gold ballpoint.

"It may take time for him to regain full control of his left side, but feeling in the muscles may come back any day." The ballpoint revolves and taps. "Or it may never come back."

She tries to stop the gold pen against the horn-rims before the doctor repeats that last sentence, but somehow his pale lips always manage to add those words before she can silence him, the way the afterglow of their TV persists when she clicks off the set.

Does CW have enough straws for his Pepsis?

She isn't sure, and she frowns along the grocery aisle, looking for drinking straws.

The left half of CW's mouth stays slack, and syrupy foam spills down his chin if he doesn't have a straw.

There are, of course, no aids to help him chew the soda crackers.

She rubs her itching wrist, falters among the paper plates, and picks up the six-pack on her way to the check-out.

She reminds herself to explain to CW how the percentages work and how when she reaches a hundred, she'll get that extra $2.53 an hour. CW would never have thought sewing would make that kind of money, and she hopes he'll be impressed.

She turns the pick-up off the blacktop, and dust encloses the cab, but it's too hot to roll up the truck windows, and she merely dabs at the grainy sweat on her forehead.

The seat, the windshield, the steering wheel are powdered with the same fine grit before she reaches the fence to the land CW bought to run cattle. No cows are left, of course, but Toby needs the barbed wire to keep him from wandering off, so she doesn't begrudge stopping to get the gate.

As she finally brakes in the hard ruts beside the trailer, she can see Toby pressed against the weathered shed door, studying her through a gap as she comes toward him.

His blond mane has been clipped into an inch-high roach, all but the wire-harsh bangs, to give him the look of a lean-faced rock singer on TV. She touches the space between the slats as she unlocks the door with her other hand, and his nose and rubbery lips come up to meet her fingers before he nudges the latch. When she works up to a hundred percent, she'll start buying him sacks of sweet feed again.

"For now you'll have to make do with summer fescue," she says as if she's mentioned the corn-grain-molasses mixture to him. "But it won't take long. I got the hang of it and all I need is practice."

She shakes her head guiltily and pats his neck. She hasn't meant to say anything to him before she's carried the day's events and the crackers and sodas to CW. Once she's mentioned the work or the women to Toby, the words are no longer fresh. "And Lord knows, poor CW needs something fresh in that room," she whispers against the pony's smooth hide.

She stokes his nose again, returns to the pick-up for the plastic grocery bag, and tells herself it'll be a relief to get out of the heat.

But her sneakers climb sluggishly up the steps to the trailer door and she sees the exposed blocks beneath the axle and trailer supports. They have the same cheap dun paint as the walls in the factory. This summer CW aimed to put skirting around the trailer and build them a tiny porch with a railing, but now—

She opens the door, and the odor overpowers her.

The air-conditioned smell is nothing she can pin down, just an odor of sick, as if helplessness gives off its own vapors.

"That you, Dell?" It's CW's voice, but not the voice he once had.

"I stopped to pick up some Pepsi. I thought you were about out," as if he's noticed she's late.

But it's mere ritual, the forced cheerfulness, the implication that he might notice her tardiness. He doesn't seem interested in anything any more, neither the time of day, nor her departures and arrivals.

"There now, how you feeling?" She peers in the bedroom door.

He doesn't resemble CW any longer either.

He hasn't for some time, but she's still newly startled each time by the partitioned face, one half twitching, the other half frozen, that looks at her from the pillow. One eye, blue and white glass, stares straight ahead while the drawn cheek and rigid mouth sag toward his jaw line. The other eye follows her, and that half of the lips stays tight and angry. The hair over both sides of his forehead hangs strangely unyielding as if it, too, is paralyzed.

"Turn that dan thing off," he says irritably in the voice that isn't his. "You know how I hate gane shows," he adds as if she's been there all afternoon watching with him.

Her reddened fingers find the remote, and she wills herself to ignore the fact that he can no longer say 'm.'

"You want a Pepsi? I got cold ones, and boy did they sweat on the way home. You wouldn't believe how hot it is out there."

The porcelain eye stares into her head, and she realizes how Gladys must have felt when she was working at Campbell Soup and playing around on her husband and having to bring home excuses and meaningless conversation every evening.

Then the unblinking eye is pulled away toward the wall beside her as CW twists the other half of his face toward the bedside table. "I could use a drink," he says.

The meekness is somehow more terrible than the irritation.

"I got up more speed today." She goes into the kitchen and her faked heartiness echoes against the metal cabinets. "When I get that hundred percent, we'll celebrate."

She carries the open soda can and the straw, a red-striped candy cane of a straw, to CW and continues with details that need no response while she gathers up wadded cracker wrappers, empty red-white-and-blue cans that CW has tried to crush with one hand.

"You want this on again?"

She clicks the button, and an announcer's enthusiasm, no less false than her own, fills the cramped room.

She carries the enameled bedpan out the kitchen door.

Toby raises his head to watch her.

"You and I'll celebrate with a race along the river," she says softly. "With the water down, you can run a good mile in shallows no deeper than your ankles. You can skim over the river pebbles as smooth as a grass carp."

She empties the container, but she stands and talks in a low voice to the pony until shadows reach across the clearing and ease up the paint-chipped sides of the trailer.

The next morning, she can tell, as she matches sleeves to jacket vests and sews, that she's getting faster.

That afternoon, she's not afraid to let the wall clock shimmer at the edge of her sight, and by quitting time, she's picked up another half a jacket.

One more sleeve, and she'll be doing eleven jackets in forty-eight minutes. Only another set in another four minutes and an additional $2.53 an hour will show up on her pale green paycheck.

The anticipation she feels gets her through the evening with more authentic cheer, and she and CW watch a comedy show with jokes funny enough for her to glance at him and for him to laugh with one side of his mouth in genuine amusement.

The following morning, she drops another thirty seconds, and by her lunch break, she tosses an eleventh jacket onto the cart in forty-eight minutes.

But during the afternoon, doubt creeps in as she throws a jacket over her shoulder. Is it as good as the ones she did when she first started? Has her machine remained as sure while she's picked up speed? Or are the rapid seams just enough off the mark to make the sleeves pull loose?

But, of course, she can't stop to check. Examining a sleeve would be as foolish as pausing for an unnecessary trip to the bathroom.

She flings the jacket over her shoulder, grabs another sleeve and begins again.

Making certain the seams hold is someone else's job anyway.

She kneads her itching arms as she leaves the building. The reddened flesh is swollen, but she doesn't mention it to CW as she tells him brightly about the older woman with the loose reptilian skin whose name is Caramel and who's perpetually afraid the company will ship the factory overseas.

"She makes doll clothes at night for extra money. I don't know how she can face a sewing machine at home after sitting behind one all day at work." She slips his empty Pepsi can away before he tries to crush it. "I sure couldn't."

She rubs one arm against the other, wants to claw at the rash. Some of the women pull old socks with the ends cut out over their arms, but CW's socks are so stained.

"I never heard of a name like Caramel, did you?"

CW doesn't answer.

He's as listless as she's ever seen him, and she suspects she shouldn't talk about work. She wouldn't if she had anything else to talk about, but she can't bring up the fences or the trailer skirting or anything else on the fifteen acres, and since there's only her grandmother left out of her folks and her grandmother doesn't do anything but watch TV all day herself, there's nothing she can say about her. CW hasn't seen his dad since he was four years old or his mother after she remarried and moved to Kerrville. It wasn't important that they didn't have family close before, but now—

She pulls back from that thought and tries to get into the TV show. Two cars are careening along a freeway, but she's missed who the drivers are or why they're chasing each other. She doesn't want to invite a spittled explanation from CW, so she keeps her face toward the screen without focusing.

Tomorrow or the next day she'll get the hundred percent. A sack of sweet feed for Toby and a surprise of some sort for CW will perk them all up.

And in her determination, only three days later she hurls a twelfth jacket onto the cart in exactly forty-eight minutes. She can't contain her smile.

The next jacket lands on top of the last in four minutes flat.

She does it with all twelve, and then twelve more.

And as the lunch buzzer sounds, she scratches her arms, smiles and waves at the checker.

"I told you when you started you could do it, didn't I?" The checker counts the jackets on the cart and smiles, too.

No one has told her how good it would feel, but then maybe nobody else married before they finished tenth grade. Or maybe they've all worked out for so long they don't remember such an initial accomplishment.

She goes eagerly to the break room, but before she can burst out with her news, Caramel looks up from her gray-filled sandwich. "Fran got canned this morning. Couldn't make more than fifty percent on buttonholes."

Dell locates the cup with her scarlet D and lets coffee trickle into it from the huge cylindrical pot.

"Those asshole managers do it every time."

The other women nod in gloomy silence and no one offers a conversational wedge for her to tell of her success. She knows they'd be as pleased for her as they are sorry for the dismissed Fran, and as she bites into the peanut and jelly sandwich that has a lingering odor of CW's bedside, she realizes she was counting on their congratulations to offset CW's apathy.

But she plucks at the sandwich and consoles herself with the thought that she can tell them on her afternoon break.

It's a shame Toby can't express the understanding she knows he has.

She files out with the rest into the great tan room, but as she reaches her machine, she sees the checker sitting on her stool.

The machines nearby whir steadily.

"We need you in buttonholes," the checker says without looking at her directly. "One of the girls in buttonholes quit this morning." She glances toward the end of the room where the buttonholers sit.

"I—I'm in sleeves."

But even as she steadies herself with a hand against the table, she sees that the sleeves and jacket halves are no longer beside her machine.

"The foreman says we're ahead on sleeves. We don't need no one on them right now. We need somebody on buttonholes."

She already knows it's no use. The checker hasn't faced her and is using 'we,' which she recognizes is a cover. But she nonetheless says, "I'm good on sleeves."

"None of them jackets can go out without buttons or buttonholes."

"I got my hundred percent. I earned an extra $2.53 an hour."

The checker starts down the aisle and says over her shoulder, "The foreman said to tell you you'd get the extra for the whole day even though you won't be doing that good the rest of the afternoon. Wouldn't hurt to thank him next time you see him."

Needles jab evenly into coarse jean material as she follows the checker.

"Somebody'll be right here to show you how to work the buttonholer."

A great pile of nearly finished jackets mounds beside the machine. The row of stools is at the far end of the room from the clock, but she can still see the electric jerking of the scarlet hand. She tries to look away, but the blue of CW's fixed eye looms out at her from the vast sand-colored wall.

THE HAT

Drought had lowered the Mississippi enough for gulf salt to emulsify its way nearly to the French Quarter and for the rotten hulk of a Civil War steamer to be exposed on the riverbank above Baton Rouge. The brick sidewalks were kilned again in the July sun, and undulating ribbons of heat slowed the stride of even the heartiest native.

She hunched against the itching sweat at her hairline and thought as she passed the wrought-iron railing of the Cathedral garden that the white stone Christ appeared to be extending his marble sleeves to dry his armpits. And she speculated as she glanced down Pirates' Alley why the glum artist pressed into his campstool hadn't had the business foresight to hang out an oil reproduction of evening Spanish moss or a misty bayou. He might have made a sale. But no panting tourist would stop for one of his clowns whose hot primary red and blue balloons beamed as hard as tin in the sun.

She gave the plate glass window beyond the alley the same cursory glance.

That was when she saw the hat.

She caught the step she'd been about to take and stopped.

The crimson sweep of straw blossomed from the Victorian hat stand with the gallant disdain of a 1940s movie. Scarlet lace, a cerise foam of red fern, and one red rose crested the brim.

It was the kind of elegant hat she'd needed for decades.

Of course, the discreet price tag dangled discreetly inward.

She planed the perspiration from her eyebrows with a forefinger and opened the shop door to a cheery bell much like that a plantation lady might once have jangled to summon afternoon tea.

The tall African American young man behind the counter bobbed his head in her direction, and his gold earring—in the shape of a Voodoo fish skeleton with attached head and tail—wriggled gold glints at her. "May I help you?"

Cinnamon pot-pourri cloyed the shop air, but the room was cool.

"I'd like to see the red straw hat in the window."

"Ah." He beamed at her. "You picked the one item in this shop with class."

He went to the window, pushed aside the gauzy drape and adroitly unhooked the hat from the stand while he scooped up a belt from the piecrust table that shared the window with the hat rack. As he reached into and withdrew from the plate glass light, she noticed that the back of his hand, the color of cloves, and his turquoise silk shirt glimmered with the same intensity.

His upraised fingertips carried the hat to the counter while his other hand spread the belt out on the glass top. "See what I mean?" He gestured with long slender fingers whose nails were buffed alabaster ovals.

She looked down at the leather belt studded with blue, green, red and yellow discs the size of quarters. They reminded her of the painted balloons in Pirates' Alley.

"Would you believe those are actually authentic topazes, garnets, aquamarines, and tourmalines?" His tone and fingers curled with aversion. "It costs $450, and it's a piece of trash. He floated the hat gently over the counter. "This is only $540, and look at the difference."

He said the sum casually as if it could be paired with 'only,' and she smiled his exemplary salesmanship.

"It's one of a kind. See how the singed peacock feathers in vermilion and the dyed French broomstraw set off the rose?" He lowered his voice even though no one else was in the shop. "I think I've been saving it especially for you."

He swirled around the polished glass counter, repositioned a salt-and-pepper curl on her sweaty forehead and tilted the hat over her hair. He stepped back, adjusted the brim a fraction of an inch, then turned her to face the mirror. "Now look. Isn't that marvelous on you?"

He was right.

The hat on her was stunning.

And it had obviously been designed with her face in mind.

The upthrust of crimson straw revealed her features as aristocratic, classic and regal, yet daring. Beneath the red silk rose in its nest of crimson down, she stood tall and imperial, no longer a mid-sized, too-thin doctor's wife, but a queenly woman whose maturity allowed her to wear red.

"I knew the right woman would come in for that lovely hat sooner or later. And now watch this." His silk arms surrounded her as he reset the hat with the rose over her left ear. "It can be worn with the blossom either in the front or on the side." He smiled at their mirror images. "And they were both made just for you."

The hat with its scarlet fantasy bloom—and her own face beneath it—were unbelievably becoming.

"Something with this taste and style never goes out of fashion. It's the essence of class. You probably shouldn't think of it as a hat but as an investment."

"We don't buy our hats; we *have* our hats," she murmured, quoting from an ancient punch line as she glanced from his appreciative eyes to study herself in the silvered glass. Although she remembered exactly the figure he'd quoted, she said, "And how much did you say it was?"

"Five hundred and forty plus tax." His clove and peach colored index finger tapped her shoulder. "But since I know it has to be yours, I can make it $525 and still break even. It's the one time I'm sure I can make the manager understand."

She gave him an answering smile in the mirror. "Can I have that in writing? I'm lunching with a friend at Galatoire's at twelve, and that'll give me time to think it over."

His reflected image behind her produced the merest semblance of a wink. "Just ask for Charles. I never go back on a bargain."

She knew Lloyd wouldn't care if she spent $525 or $540 plus tax on a hat if she wanted the hat, and although she knew the young man was right and that the hat had indeed been made for her, she hadn't walked into the Fleur de Paris shop prepared to hand over that kind of money, and she couldn't bring herself to buy it on the spot. If her impulse lasted overnight, she'd return in the morning.

But she couldn't stop herself from saying. "Could you not display it in the window right away?"

"Certainly. I know you have to own this hat, Mrs.—?"

"Hamilton. Bea Hamilton."

And when she opened the door to the anvil heat of Royal Street, she was nearly certain she'd return for the matchless, one-of-a-kind crimson hat.

She hoarded the memory of her transformation under the red silk rose on her walk to Galatoire's, and while she waited at the table for Irene, she wondered what the brown and peach and turquoise young man did when he wasn't behind the counter at the Fleur de Paris boutique.

Silken Charles. He might be a Tulane or a Dillard student, or, with his aplomb, he could be a performer at some club in the Quarter. She told herself she wasn't naïve enough to assume that he was straight. Hardly any male working in the Quarter was. But the fact that a young gay man with a discerning eye saw that the hat should belong to her was doubly complimentary. She remembered his dark approving eyes. And for a young gay black man to see her as more than just any nondescript white Garden District matron was even more—

"Have you been waiting long?" Irene wedged her bulk into a chair and fanned her flushed cheeks with the menu. "I'm starved."

Irene's 160 pounds on a bone structure meant to carry less than a hundred was always starved, and Bea let her ponder the menu without asking what she thought about spending more than $500 on a hat.

"I'm going to splurge on a giant shrimp cocktail, the pompano, asparagus tips, and an éclair," Irene said. And since she'd arrived amply equipped with stories of the drought wreaking havoc with the lawns along St. Charles and wilting all the exotics in Audubon Park, Bea didn't find an opportunity during lunch to bring up the marvelous hat or Silken Charles.

As they left the restaurant, however, she sensed a strange urgency, and she said quickly, "I want to show you something I'm considering buying," as she urged Irene's short legs to waddle faster.

"For heaven's sake, Bea, we'll both collapse with sunstroke."

They turned on Royal, and her temples thudded—not from the heat or the haste but with panic—and she castigated herself for hesitating. Despite her special look in the crimson hat, Silken Charles couldn't be expected to save it for her if some perspiring tourist from Michigan plunked down $540 plus tax for it.

Why hadn't she given him a fifty to put it back for her?

She saw immediately that the hat wasn't in the window and that a frothy yellow straw with pearlized lace and silk talisman roses balanced on the hat rack.

"Oh, look, Bea. Isn't that lovely?" Irene pointed to the multi-studded leather belt that *had* been returned to the Victorian piecrust table.

Bea didn't answer as she pushed open the door to the bell chime. The veins on the back of her thin hand protruded with tension.

Silken Charles lounged behind the counter.

He smiled at her, then let his smile include Irene coming through the door.

Bea hadn't noticed before how many ruby-hued items lined the shelves, and her gaze faltered. "Is that red hat—?"

What if it were gone?

If it had been sold would they create another?

Then she saw it.

Swinging from a hook above a raspberry stole, it glistened in candy apple red.

She caught her breath with relief as Irene came up beside her. She knew she'd buy the wonderful hat whether Irene approved or not.

"Yes, the gorgeous red straw." Silken Charles sprang toward the hat and lifted it with his beautifully expressive hands.

"I can't believe how long it's been since I stopped in here," Irene was saying. "I love that belt you have in the window with all the jewels."

But Bea didn't glance aside from the polished French straw and the startling true-red silk rose—which could be worn over one ear or in the center of her forehead—borne aloft in Silken Charles's cinnamon hands with their tea-rose fingernails.

"This is simply the finest hat we've ever made here in the shop," he said as he swept it carefully onto Irene's white hair and turned her toward the mirror. "Now look. Isn't that marvelous on you?"

DELETING DEREK

He props his right foot and work boot beside him on the kitchen chair and unfastens the meticulously tied leather laces. And although he doesn't glance at his fingers, he begins stretching the thong in even increments from the eyelets until the tongue loosens enough to free his foot in its heavy gray sock. He stands that boot erect on the floor and lifts his left foot to the plastic seat. All without looking away from his wife who is laughing into the phone across the kitchen.

Through her laugh she says, "You could load it that way all right, but warn me when you do so I can duck when the board starts spitting parts all over the room." She pauses for a response, laughs again.

The left work boot has been as deliberately removed before she says, "Well, I got to go make supper for Loy," and both boots, their steel toes together, have been aligned with the linoleum border before she finally hangs up.

"You're encouraging him, talking to him after work like that."

"Come on, Loy." She produces a grin obviously intended to reassure. "I'm pushing fifty. From the other direction."

"Young guys like him don't call two, three times a week unless they got a fantasy going. Especially they don't call some woman they see at the next machine all day."

"He's still new at Baldwin. He just needs to talk to some old lady who knows the ropes."

"Six months ain't new."

"Come on, Loy, Derek's younger than Tony."

"Look how many old geezers marry women young as their daughters—or even their granddaughters."

"Well, he's getting married to Paula next month." She bends for a frying pan and says to the stove, "And she's twenty-two as well."

"That don't mean squat."

She tilts a block of worm-pink ground round into the skillet. "I never heard such nonsense."

"You don't know how guys think," he says stubbornly.

She snorts derisively, lets the grease spatter substitute for an answer.

And only after she's filled the plates and dealt them onto two unraveling cotton placemats does she look at him. She bounces her chair under the table and tells him how the last shipment of minuscule parts arrived without spools, how the minute pegs skittered into every corner of the unopened boxes.

"How they put up with that kind of shoddy delivery I'll never know. Derek says I ought to bid for manager next time."

Loy frowns over his loaded tines of Hamburger Helper, but as if she hasn't noticed, she goes on about one of the plant managers who stood directly under the yellow warning placard, NO FOOD OR DRINK IN THIS AREA, and sipped his coffee.

"I told him if he was going to have coffee there, he could bring me a cup next time and he could take down the sign. But if there was a reason nobody ought to drink beside our machines, then maybe he ought to go to the break room."

He slants his fork across the empty plate. "What'd he say?"

"He looked like a three-year-old caught with his hand in the cookie jar and bounded off. Everybody tried to keep from laughing, but I bet he won't bring coffee back in the work area again."

Derek isn't mentioned again during the evening's TV, he doesn't telephone while Loy's home for the next week, and reference to him comes only obliquely when she exhibits the towels she's bought for Paula's wedding shower.

"You never know what colors to get, but Target had these green ones that don't look too shabby."

"Why does girl who has to get married want a shower?"

"They need house wares, too," she says shortly.

He shrugs.

Then, three days before the wedding, during the final story of the late news, the phone rings.

As she answers Derek's voice says without preamble, "If you weren't thirty years too old, I'd have asked you to marry me next weekend."

She emits a startled chuckle.

"Why'd you have to be old enough to be my mother?"

But it's not a question, and she forces the chuckle again. "Or maybe your grandmother. Remember, we marry young in the country."

"What would you have said?"

This *is* a question, a serious one, demanding considerations, and she laughs. "If I weren't thirty years too old, that is." But when his silence rejects the sidestep, she adds, "Maybe I'd of said 'yes.'"

"Why'd you have to be old?" He hangs up.

She takes the receiver from her ear and stares at it as Loy appears in the kitchen. "What was that all about?"

"I think he had a couple of beers."

"I told you not to encourage him."

She presses the phone stirrup silent. "I work with the kid. That's all."

"But you'd marry him if you was thirty years younger."

"Oh, you heard that on the extension? Good grief, Loy. I got a thirty-year cushion. He's a nice kid. What's the harm in giving him a compliment?"

"If that don't sound encouraging, I don't know what does."

"Oh, come off it."

"I'm telling you, you don't know how guys' minds work."

"He's probably just got the jitters about the wedding."

"All I'm saying is—"

She strides from the kitchen, kicking his boots askew as she passes. When he snaps off the TV and comes to bed, neither of them says anything.

Two nights later, Derek calls, but he makes no reference to his previous conversation, and she says she has to hang up and throw some cracked corn to her hens before Loy drives up. They don't talk on the phone again until after the J.P. wedding at the courthouse, and then the call is only a brief query to see if she knows a good doctor because Paula isn't happy with the one she's got.

As they sit down to the Papa John's pepperoni pizza she's brought home since she's worked overtime, she says to Loy, "There's so much kids have to contend with these days what with all the drugs and the lay-offs and AIDS and all."

"You thinking about Tony and his girl?"

"No. Just kids in general."

The next few calls from Derek are infrequent and businesslike.

Until a month later.

At 2 a.m.

She leaps from the bed, sprints across the icy linoleum to grab the phone. But as she utters a panicked "Hello" a male voice begins to sing, "I love you. I love you" to the accompaniment of a clumsy guitar.

"What is it? Something happen to Tony?" Loy calls from the bedroom.

She covers the receiver. "No. It's not Tony."

"What is it?" He comes up beside her and listens. Then he takes the phone and hangs up. "Was that Derek?"

"I couldn't tell. Whoever it was sounded sloshed."

"It was him."

"I don't know."

The telephone shrills again, and they both jump.

She starts to pick it up, but Loy stays her hand, and after four rings, her voice on the answering machine says brightly, "We're not home right now, but leave a message and your number and we'll get back to you as soon as we can."

After a slight pause, the guitar begins again, and the male voice sings softly, "I love you. I love you. I love you," until the allotted time on the machine clicks off.

When no more calls come, they go back to bed.

But the next morning before work, Loy jabs the PLAY button. The awkward strumming and the tuneless phrases fill the kitchen.

"That him?"

"Like I say, I can't tell."

"Who else would be calling you at 2 a.m. and singing a love song?"

"You call that singing?"

"That's what comes of encouraging him."

"This is the stupidest conversation I ever heard." She grabs her sack lunch, purse, truck keys, and slams out the back door.

That night after work as they sit down to eat, Loy presses the PLAY tab.

"I love you. I love you. I love you" drowns the click of stainless forks against the Melmac. She glowers at Loy and at the answering machine, but she doesn't say anything to either.

When what is ostensibly a song is silenced once more, Loy says, "When are you going to delete that?"

"You delete it."

He glares. "You encouraged him."

"You're the one who's jealous."

"He's singing to you."

"How do you know? Maybe it's one of the guys out at the site who saw you in that khaki shirt with your name on the pocket and was hoping you'd be the one to answer the phone at 2 a.m."

He turns a shocked expression toward her. Then, "It's Derek."

She shrugs. "I don't know that."

He thumbs the button again, and they both sit and look at the answering machine as it runs.

He plays it again before they go to bed.

"Why don't you just delete it?" she says.

"It's up to you. He's smitten with you."

"Like I say, you're the one who's jealous."

The recording is replayed nightly, other messages follow until the illuminated numbers under the plastic window of the answering machine tack into double digits.

And still the voice sings to the background guitar, "I love you. I love you. I love you."

THE GOLD-LEAFED GIRL

The graceful young woman who steps from the moonlit deck into the cruise ship dining room is someone the other passengers are forced to notice if for no other reason than that she glitters as if she's been freshly dusted with gold. A gilded turban obscures her hair and lends a metallic sheen to her flaxen eyebrows, a high-collared gold lamé dress swirls knee-length to reveal legs in sheer golden-spangled hose, and a pair of gold sequined pumps twinkle their burnished heels as she radiates toward the captain's table. She carries a gold link evening bag in a hand whose nails have been lacquered with fourteen-karat polish, and when she reaches the edge of the white tablecloth, she winks at the captain across the candle flames.

"How are you feeling this morning, honey?" the man's words overlap the click of crystal goblets on the captain's table, obscure the strings of the ship's orchestra.

She slowly angles her green irises and pupils in his direction, and although he's still too far from the bed to appear in her line of vision, she blinks twice, her affirmative for 'Yes' or 'Fine' or 'All right,' and he says cheerfully, "That's good," exactly the way he says it every morning.

He moves into range. "It's going to be a hot one," he adds as he does nearly every day between April and October.

He wears a tee-shirt that has been thrown repeatedly into a laundromat washer with jeans, black socks, and her assorted nightgowns until its color has set into a shade of sodden gray, but his cheeks glisten, closely shaven, and he smells of Brut astringent.

"They're sending some social worker out to check on Erin, but you don't need to worry. They'll see he's right as rain."

She lowers and raises her lashes twice.

But he may not have noticed since he's wedging his wrists under her armpits to lift her and drop her forward onto his chest while he stows pillows behind her back. He's done the maneuver so often that her inert arms and legs should be easy for him to adjust into their morning incline, but the core of her bones has hardened rock solid, and he struggles as he did the first morning he arranged her body without the help of a nurse.

"You ready for some breakfast?"

She blinks once, but he's already left the bedroom for the trailer kitchen and the eggs he scrambled earlier.

In the cruise ship lounge, the golden girl with the laughing green eyes and the golden turban swirls into the rhythm of a tango.

Her husband re-enters with a saucer of eggs, sits heavily on the bed, and smooths back greasy strands of hair that had once been Clairol honey blond. "Here we are."

Her expression holds a serene half smile as if her bodily decay halted the facial muscles in mid-pleasantry, and he now opens the upturned lips to place a tiny clot of blended yolk and white on her tongue.

As he gently works the lump of egg toward her esophagus and her gag reflex brings it forward again, his fingers massage her neck to force a swallow. He talks as he watches the progress of the bite, telling her he's repaired the eighteen inch TV and that he'll start on the twenty-two inch that afternoon. He occasionally asks if she needs a dropper of water or if she remembers Mrs. Watkins who'd left him her cheap toaster to fix simply because she didn't want to make the effort to shop for a new one—questions that can be answered with one blink or two—but mostly he explains how he discovered the short that was charring the Watkins' toast, and how he found a refrigerator at a garage sale that contained at least twice the paid sum in usable parts.

After an hour, when half the cold egg crumbles have disappeared, either down her throat or onto the ruffle of her gown, he asks, "How's that?" and at her double blink, he says, "We'll get you cleaned up now for the social worker. Let's hope it's a woman."

It is.

A round-faced young woman in a dusty red car who drives up, brakes, and waits for the grit cloud to colloid into the air so she can study the trailer with its phalanx of broken stoves, dryers, dishwashers.

At last she lifts the clipboard off the passenger seat, re-checks the number on the dented mailbox, and opens the car door.

Two sheets of particle board overlap on the dirt in a makeshift sidewalk between the sentinel appliances, and a 4 x 8 cut of thick plywood slants a wheelchair ramp to the trailer door. There's no other entry access, and her sandals pound a disquieting thud as she climbs the plywood incline.

"Hello?" she calls through the screen door.

"Be right there," a man's voice answers at once.

But nothing moves inside the trailer.

Although the blinds have been pulled against the sun, moted residual light inside the front room reveals stacked televisions, gape-doored microwaves, small electrical units whose original use is no longer apparent.

She waits, but no one acknowledge her further, and she wipes perspiration from her forehead. The pages on her clipboard wilt.

Finally she calls again, "Hello?"

"Be right there."

And this time, a short, slightly paunchy, clean-shaven and ruddy-faced man does appear at the screen.

"Come in. But watch your step. I got this trailer cheap, and you could see why if it wasn't so dark." He speaks with the linked heartiness of someone who habitually engages in one-sided conversations. "My wife's in here."

The young woman follows him through the maze of enameled hulls into a room that contains an abundance of bright yellow sunlight but that smells of human secretions and caked medicinal spoons.

"This is the lady from Health and Human Services I told you about this morning," he says to the immobile woman on the bed.

Records in the Austin office document that he's just turned thirty-six, that his wife will be thirty-nine, but they're both so blanched and clotted, like glass in the early stages of empurpling in the sun, that it's difficult to tell their ages, and she averts her eyes from the bed as she grasps her pen and clipboard with sweaty fingers. "Who helps out when you're at work?"

"I work at home. I repair appliances."

She doesn't look up or glance at the bed. "Our records indicate that you're an engineer."

"I majored in mechanical engineering in college. I worked my way through school as an assistant to physically challenged students." He smiles fondly at the bed. "That's how we met. I pushed her wheelchair to class."

"Do you make enough repairing appliances to support a family?"

"Well, there's disability, and we—" He pauses.

"Your phone's been disconnected, and your electricity is about to be turned off," she says, lowering her voice.

"I've got a couple of TVs ready to go." His tone also drops as the false cheerfulness evaporates.

"You must understand that you may be in danger of losing your child to foster care. There have been some complaints from his school, and his teacher doesn't think—"

"We had a real miracle in Erin," he murmurs. "We never thought she could get pregnant."

They're both whispering now, both avoiding a glance at the bed.

But the gold-leafed girl with the dancing green eyes, clad in a metallic gold lycra swimsuit, has just plunged into a crystalline lagoon, and the sunlit ripples are spinning triangles of beaten gold before her as her golden tanned arms and her laugh cut through the emerald water.

HAWK WOMAN AT PETERBILT

"Even the name on them things got the right sing to it," he said.

She glanced back at him with eyes the color of slag, and when she kept walking, he added, "You know, Peterbilt, built by somebody with balls."

She stopped and her stare could have crackled the space between them. "Why don't you new guys ever come up with one that ain't stale." She pulled open a door reinforced with 2 x 4 struts. "Here. This is the loading dock. The manager's Ron, over there with the bald head."

But the men had been slicking their hair, deliberately and with calculated nonchalance, to slide on their yellow hard hats, and by the time he pivoted toward the group, no bald head was visible.

"Which one?"

"Ask." She shoved her way back through the door with a disgusted shoulder. And as it wheezed shut again, she said to the hallway, "How the hell are they able to hire some ignorant asshole every damned time?"

It took longer than usual for her to reach the office since she was favoring her knee as she climbed the stairs, but when she looked down through the plate glass rectangle that overlooked the loading dock, the new man still slouched beside the door.

"Consistently," she said with the same disgust.

Then she picked up the microphone from her desk. "Ron, we got that replacement for Jay." Her words boomed in static chips from the speaker, louder than the motor of the backhoe Wilson was maneuvering up the ramp into the hauling truck, and when every face except Wilson's tipped toward her in the window, she jerked her thumb in the direction of the new employee.

His name was Briley Parker, but she didn't announce that into the cheese-grater bulb of her microphone, and instead she clicked the OFF button. "Dumb son-of-a-bitch won't be here long enough to live down that piss-ant name anyway." She pressed her kneecap with one hand and dropped into the swivel chair.

By the time the factory whistle gave the shift-changing bleat and she looked through the window again into the dock area, all the day's orange backhoes had been chained and stabilized on the carrier, and Briley Parker was indistinguishable from the others in his indistinguishable factory yellow hard hat. Her reflection, with its stiff gray perm, laced a water image over the loading platform while the men filed out, and she studied the hazy immobile woman in the glass for a few seconds before she turned to gather up her thermos and creased brown paper bag in which she'd pack her tuna sandwich and apple the next morning.

As she opened the office door, she dutifully followed the admonition above the light switch to save electricity and snapped the room into dusk.

On the way to her car, she paused to watch one of their own backhoes at work on the drainage ditch. The hinged, serrated shovel-scoop gobbled at the earth like both a nuzzling head and a fumbling paw. The metal neck with its thick cable tendons ducked and nudged, pried its saw teeth around a massive rock. The huge rock lifted momentarily, hung suspended in the half-claw of the shovel, then thudded more securely into its earthen niche.

The driver yanked the levers, threw the backhoe into reverse, accelerated again, then lowered the notched scoop toward the granite slab again.

"How long you been working that thing?" she asked in a normal tone not audible over the labored pitch of the motor. "I seen guys make them things dance."

At that moment, a hawk wheeled from the gallery forest along the highway to glide across the evening. She stared up, and her features relaxed into approval as she watched the soaring bird starkly inked against the layered amethyst sky.

She always arrived at the factory early, and the next morning she appeared a good twenty minutes before the shift began. "What am I supposed to do in an already scrubbed kitchen?" she'd say whenever one of the file girls from down the hall chided her promptness that made everyone else look bad.

Yet that morning, as early as she was, Briley Parker already lounged on the loading dock.

"What's he doing down there?"

She reached for the intercom, but as if he sensed her presence, he looked up.

"My wife just had twins," he shouted toward the second floor, and his words glittered faintly through the glass. "It's quieter here." Then he produced a smug grin and amplified his words with columned hands. "Twin boys, of course."

She turned from the window, slammed her sack into the desk drawer and, despite the spasm of pain that twisted her lips, kneed the drawer shut.

"When does an asshole like that catch on that you breed girls if you screw all the time and you produce boys if you get it only once a month?" She scowled at the computer screen as she jabbed it on. "Somebody ought to cue him in. One of these days I just might myself."

But since she ate lunch in the office rather than in the break room, she didn't see Briley Parker again until the morning of his eighth day on the job.

It was a hot morning, and she'd glanced once or twice at the rigid amber block of sunlight dropping through the ramp door, but she was tabulating invoices with her usual determination when the yelling began.

Voices bellowing, echoing from the concrete floor and cinder block walls.

She swiveled to peer down.

Briley Parker and two other men were racing in a frenzied circle while they waved their arms and enameled hats. A knot of workers near the door watched as the three of them lunged and leapt after each other in an uneven dance and fanned their hats through the cube of light. The enamel gleamed aching yellow.

She almost smiled at their antics when a black wingspan nearly a yard wide sailed from a shaded corner into the sun.

"Hey!"

The dark wings veered by the doorway, seemed about to careen into the shadowed back wall, but at the last second, banked and curved into a whirl across the sunlight.

"Hey! That's a hawk!" She grabbed the microphone.

The three workers galloped after the bird, chasing it with flapping arms and shouts.

The hawk began to brake in frantic loops, and Briley Parker flung his hat at it. The canary yellow half-sphere bounced along the concrete, but Briley Parker kept his eyes on the bird while he seized a 2 x 4 from the pile.

"Don't!"

But her cry went unheeded as Briley Parker positioned himself in a batter's stance while the other two men flailed their arms and yipped behind the wings.

"Goddamn it! It's a hawk! It's endangered!"

The 2 x 4 swung, but the bird swooped up and out of range.

When it reached the block wall, however, it had to sheer away and circle.

The 2 x 4 swung again.

A sound of cracking bone came through her glass as the wings shuddered, retracted, and a wild whoop went up.

The 2 x 4 drew back and Briley Parker bunted the hawk out the door.

The others in the chase screeched their approbation, and the three of them dashed down the loading ramp after the bird.

The men watching shook their heads as they shuffled back to work, and Wilson scowled, but she didn't move until Briley Parker came back inside, laughing and stretching his arms to spread the mangled black wings. The words with which he congratulated himself didn't reach the second floor as the fork-lift motor started.

She stared down, replaced the intercom microphone to pick up the telephone.

"I want the number of the EPA," she said, her jaw stiff, and when she punched in the number she was given, she explained stiffly that some men in her building had just killed an endangered species.

"Do you have positive evidence of that?" The question came from a female, but the query was so coolly official that the speaker could have been any gender.

Her lips formed the word 'Yes' before she said it aloud.

"We'll send someone out. Where is your building?"

After she hung up, she tilted back in her chair, not returning to the invoices but merely rocking and waiting until two men in sweaty suits and Walmart ties appeared at the office door.

From her window, she pointed out the dark form of the dead hawk while she gave the two men an unemotional explanation of the killing. After she directed them to the loading platform, she took up her thermos and left the office.

The next morning, Briley Parker was waiting in the parking lot.

"What did you have to do that for? I got a wife and a couple of kids." He thrust his head in her car window as she pulled the hand brake. "What's a hawk to you anyway?"

She pushed the button to roll up the window without looking at him. She turned the key, extracted it and placed both Air-Walkers flat on the asphalt to jack-knife from behind the steeringwheel. "Killing an endangered species is a federal offense."

"With two new babies, I can't afford no pink slip."

She slammed the car door.

"The company's got to eat the fine," he said. "No way there ain't going to be pink slips in lots of boxes this morning. Ron was still talking to the EPA when the shift ended last night."

She didn't look at him as she walked away from the car.

"We was just having a little fun."

Now she glanced at his sheepish face. "Yeah, boys will be boys. Ain't that always the case?"

His hands fell to his sides. "I got two kids."

At the entrance, she pulled open the door with its discrete frosted PETERBILT letters etched in the glass. "After you."

Although he glared at her, he slumped by and walked with a curiously childlike gait down the hall ahead of her.

"Poor son-of-a-bitch," she said softly as she followed him.

He didn't pause at the break room door and was already scanning the wall of mail cubicles when she came in.

But he'd been wrong. Only one pink slip had been stuffed aslant in one mailbox.

Hers.

The pink cardstock vibrated from the box like an erroneous mashed tropical flower, garish and misplaced in the beige room. She shot a glance at Briley Parker, but he was staring at the wall of mailboxes.

The pink slip wisped a paper sigh as she lifted it out, and three black feathers fluttered to the linoleum tiles. Her name had been typed across the top, and Ron had scribbled in the COMMENTS space: "Inability to get along with co-workers."

She stared at it.

"I been here fourteen years," she murmured.

Briley Parker still gazed in bewilderment at the wall. "I thought—"

She immediately tensed her jaw, and as her glance slid away from him, she turned her back to the row of boxes.

Then she stepped over the hawk feathers, shouldered the door open again, and strode into the hall without limping.

THE KINDNESS OF STRANGERS

She crosses her legs, which could be those of a twenty-year-old in the sheer black stockings, and tilts her chin to firm her neck. She arches a palm around the sazerac tumbler and feels for the drink straw with her tongue.

A man three stools away, with a forehead knobbed like a sack of pebbles, is gazing into the bar mirror at her, and their eyes meet in the counterfeit space beyond the glass. He watches her, then hefts his half-empty beer mug and slides onto the plastic seat next to her.

She doesn't turn but locks him in the mirror for scrutiny. He's wearing a green windbreaker with "Mel" machine-stitched on the pocket.

"You want a fresh one a them?" He indicates her glass.

She rewards him with a luminous smile. "That would be lovely."

He forks two fingers at the bartender.

"What do you do for a living, Mel?" She licks out for the straw of the fresh drink.

"Right now I'm looking for a new line a work."

She inclines one shoulder. "Aren't we all?"

She sips the licorice-flavored concoction and doesn't say she's unemployed, too, now that her divorce is final.

They drink the drinks, he orders them both another while she makes bright conversation, and when her glass reaches backwash, she says, "I've got a beer in the refrigerator if you'd like to walk me home for a nightcap."

He looks suddenly crafty and nervous, and his eyes cringe beneath the eyelids that in the gold over-the-bar-light have the appearance of tangerine rinds.

"That was what you had in mind when you sat down here, wasn't it?"

"Yes, ma'am."

"We don't have to be *that* polite in the French Quarter." She notches into sharpness, but catches herself immediately and drawls, "We don't stand on much ceremony here."

His nervous seems to increase after they step into the dark street, and she clasps his moon-slick sleeve. "I always like to hang onto something when I'm wearing heels."

She settles the purse strap on her shoulder bone.

He walks in tense silence, and the night chill and the cold fingernail of a moon swirl through her silk blouse and nylons.

When she finds the gate key in the shoulder bag, she doesn't offer it to him to do the gallant gesture, and while she pushes back the iron gate, she glances at him and sucks in her cheeks as if she's about to rescind her offer of a nightcap.

But she doesn't, and they cross the patio bricks and start up the stairs together.

His heavy tread clangs on the metal staircase and, when she stops on the balcony, his breath is just above her ear.

She unlocks the door and clicks on the overhead.

The white light is too sudden, too harsh, and she shades her face with horizontal fingers as she drops the purse on the couch and goes quickly into the kitchen. "Close the door," she calls back.

The kitchen light she doesn't turn on.

"One cold Bud coming up."

Her gaiety is strained, but she opens the can by the glimmer of moonlight from the kitchen window and waits for him to appear in the archway. When he doesn't, she adds, "I'll pour it in a goblet. I don't have any beer steins." She raises her voice for him to join her. "I think I'll have a white wine with you. Isn't there some quaint saying about how you can thwart a hangover if you go from the grain to the grape?"

A grunt, a possible negative or affirmative, comes from the living room as she opens the refrigerator, watches the bulb press on, off, and fills the wineglass from the already uncorked bottle.

She balances a crystal goblet in each hand.

The stems are heavy, octagonal, and reassuring, and since she's changed the locks, Robert can't get back in the apartment to claim them—or anything else.

"Come and get it." Her tone is also under control.

No sound comes from the living room.

"You don't have to worry." She listens, then produces a chuckle meant to be encouraging. "I haven't been with anybody for years except one very lousy-in-bed husband who ran off with his legal secretary."

She goes from the darkened kitchen into the living room glare.

She blinks, and her gaze swerves from the scrambled contents of the purse to the empty space beside the couch where the TV had been.

She stands totally still a moment before she says softly, "The son of a bitch."

The two lead crystal glasses and their eight-sided stems begin to sweat in her hands.

"The sons of bitches." Her voice solidifies with caustic satisfaction. "The goddamned sons of bitches."

THE STAND-OFF

Miss Braddock apparently considered it a rebellion she had to quell.

What else would it be coming from the best all-around student in the eighth grade? What else from the student all the teachers knew would earn an A or even an A+ in whatever subject they were teaching because the girl's father expected nothing less?

It started with a straightforward six-weeks' test.

"All right, girls, seven balls over the net. We begin swim classes next week, so let's get this show on the road and finish our volleyball requirements. Seven out of ten and you're proficient enough for a C. So try to do better."

The rumor was that she'd come straight from the army to Lakehill Academy and hence identified students by the surnames stenciled on their white gym shirt pockets. The other persistent rumor was that she disliked teaching because she was either a professional tennis player or golfer in that other life and that she could have been world class if she'd remained in whichever sport she played.

"Chisholm, you and Hudson and Lattimore start."

The class dutifully lined up behind the three girls, who toed the red out-of-bounds border painted on the gym floor and swung their arms back in unison. Three fists simultaneously cracked the three leather orbs that arched with smart precision over the net.

The girls in line clapped, and although Miss Braddock on the other side of the net didn't applaud, she nonetheless lobbed the balls back with a satisfied toss.

Barbara Chisholm sent the next nine of her balls over with ease before she bowed and trotted to the bleachers to sit out the rest of the class period. Laura Lattimore served one ball too low, and it lunged back on her side of the net, but Kim Hudson slammed hers across for an easy ten out of ten.

All three made it look effortless, and when Sally, Jenna, and Pug replaced them on the boundary line, they were accompanied with relaxed and cheerful banter.

"Okay, quit horsing around. Let's finish up so we can get in the pool on Monday."

Despite scattered giggles and a few cat-calls whenever someone missed two balls in a row, the servers moved up, one after the other, at a good clip. Most of the class had blasted eight or nine balls over the net and had retreated to the bleachers before half the hour elapsed.

The un-athletic girls herded toward the back where they usually spent their gym periods, waiting unobtrusively, listening for the bell, hoping to avoid notice and performance. But that afternoon, performance was mandatory, and the girl at the end of the line watched while everyone managed to whiz enough balls over the net.

Until only two more girls waited nervously ahead of her.

Amy Simmons got only six of the ten over, and Miss Braddock called in a bored voice, "Okay, watch what you're doing. Try another ten, Simmons."

On the next attempt, Amy made her seven, Frances Whittle moved up and met the requirement after three tries.

Finally, only the last girl remained.

Her first ball dove directly into the net, stretched it forward like a pliant web woven by a giant arachnid. The ball hung a few seconds before it tumbled to the floor.

A few companionable giggles came from the bleachers, but most of the class sat listless, ready for the period to end. Watching everyone serve, watching Miss Braddock chase and return balls had ceased to interest anyone.

Even Miss Braddock appeared ready to send them to the showers and she gave the girl a perfunctory, "Come on, Morgan, just hit it."

The girl pulled back her arm and struck her roll of thumb and fingers against the leather.

The ball flew under the net toward Miss Braddock's unshaven legs.

She sidestepped, punted the ball back, and the girl gathered it to try again.

This time the ball tipped the canvas strip at the top of the net as it dropped over.

"That's a net ball, Morgan. It doesn't count." She scooped it up and tossed it. "As soon as you get your act together, we can all go to the showers. Chisholm here wants extra time to do her hair."

Her eyes turned glacial gray as she moved closer to the net to retrieve the next few balls until at last one ball managed to zoom across—without snagging the top of the net. Miss Braddock danced backward to reach it in the air and slap it across the net. "Well, so you've decided to pass this test after all."

But that ball had been an accident.

And the next half dozen plowed into the net again.

The bleachers became breathlessly silent. All eyes followed the balls passing back and forth. Each ball that hit the net and dropped plunged into a vast pool of sympathy.

Again. And again.

Then abruptly the warning bell sounded.

"All right, the rest of you go get dressed. Morgan, what's your next class?"

"English."

"I'm sure you've got an A in English." She didn't wait for confirmation. "I'm sending a note with Lattimore that you're working with me next period."

The others filed out silently, their sneakers padding down the bleacher rows.

Barbara Chisholm stopped beside the girl, took her hand—which had become an angry red—and carefully bent the fingers and thumb into the proper serve position. "If you clench your fist like this, it may give you more control."

"Go on, Chisholm, beat it." Miss Braddock frowned. "I know you don't have an A in your next class. You can't afford to miss it, whatever it is."

Barbara Chisholm swung away, and the girl stood until Laura Lattimore returned from the dressing room and reluctantly accepted the note Miss Braddock scribbled on a pass slip.

The next class straggled in, but Miss Braddock waved them off the floor and into the bleachers. "You all wait until Morgan here decides to hit seven balls over the net."

The girls sat, talked, glanced occasionally without interest at the gym floor, and when the bell rang, Miss Braddock said, "Okay, settle down. Give Morgan a chance to concentrate. It won't take her long now that she knows I mean business."

She was wrong, of course.

But it didn't take the newly arrived class long to realize they were witnessing something they hadn't often—if ever—seen, a contest in which the odds on both sides had become insurmountable.

Once, halfway through the period, two balls in a row sailed across the net, and the watchers heaved a wavering sigh containing palpable encouragement that a streak might be starting, that the next eight balls might allow five to fall on the opposite side of the net.

They didn't.

No one in the bleachers moved.

The girls huddled together, willing the next ball, or the next, to clear the fissile-woven diamonds that hung between the two contestants.

The pad of the girl's hand began to empurple.

"Miss Braddock, could I show her how to—?" someone asked from the stands.

"No! Just sit there!"

Miss Braddock threw another ball to the girl.

She missed it.

She picked it up, and when she sent it back, it snuggled into the net a moment before it loosened itself and fell to the waxed floor.

The warning bell sounded.

"What's your next class, Morgan?"

"Geometry."

And now neither of their voices sounded familiar.

Some of the girls left the bleachers to crowd around the girl and give her quick pointers, and their advice mingled with clucks of commiseration before they were ordered away. One of them was directed to take a note to the geometry teacher.

At the next bell, the next class poured in to fill the bleachers and wait for seven out of ten balls to clear the net.

But this hour the girls sat alert, as if they'd already heard about what was happening in the gym.

"All right, Morgan." Miss Braddock pitched a ball, and one of the watching girls stepped onto the floor, grabbed it, and handed it to the girl.

"Go back and sit down, Peterson. And stay there!"

"But she's trying."

"I said sit down!" She sent another ball over the net toward the girl.

It bounced, and the girl caught it against her chest.

She balanced it on her left hand and slammed it as hard as she could with her swollen right fist.

The bleachers held a collective breath.

The ball hit the net, rested briefly in the webbing, then thudded to the floor.

NINE HUNDRED AND THIRTY ACRES

One

"It's rightfully mine." Her lacquered fingertips caught her scowl, and she reshaped her face into lines of astonishment, an expression which a beautician once assured her would tighten muscles against aging. "I can't help it if old Faye Dunlap fell in love and cut them two fat sons of his out of his will."

"Billy Todd ain't fat." Carlotta slouched on a sewing rocker, in which no female from the family had sewn since 1859, and pointed the toes of her hightops.

"His kind of twenty-year-old pork turns to a barrel of lard just like J.R. when he hits forty." She examined her size seven dandelion gold suit in the "pier glass," which she insisted on calling it, and tapped her hard-sprayed dandelion gold curls. "Nobody'd guess I was forty-eight, would they? You got to admit Faye had good taste."

"I heard Willamena wasn't much of a prize."

"Willamena Dunlap died the year you was born, Miss Sass." But her tone was indifferent. "She was a real beauty in her day."

"They called anybody a beauty who didn't have a face full of smallpox scars."

"You read that in some book?" It wasn't a real question, however, and she went on at once. "It ain't my

---

fault Faye wasn't in tip-top shape after all the wedding fuss, and—"

"Does that mean 'after all that sex'?"

"—and that his poor old heart just give plumb out."

Two

The air hung as thick as sacking in the courtroom, and spectators wore the pinched expressions of people inhaling an oily mix of perspiration laced with linseed polish. Although most of them remained curious about the outcome of the case, most had also begun to peer at their watches.

Carlotta sat behind her grandmother's yellow suit at the defendant's table and pressed her knees against the banister. She crossed her arms, and the curve of her shoulder blades indicated to the back rows that she was one of the few in the room who didn't give a damn who got the disputed nine hundred and thirty acres.

The bulbous giant in the witness box had no such curve to his spine and was repeating, "—in less than six weeks. If there ain't something suspicious in a man hearty as a bull keeling over in his breakfast eggs—"

Judge Harlan lifted his palm and shoved at the dense air. "That ain't in the considering, J.R. This is a hearing to decide one thing—if the new Mrs. Dunlap is entitled to old Faye's land."

"It's been our land since before I was born." His huge cheeks and chins distended with anger and his massive fingers clenched.

"The question before the court is whose land it'll be tomorrow," the judge said mildly, and when someone in the courtroom coughed a laugh, he frowned. "That'll do."

Then he called Amos Allworthy, old Faye's lawyer, who at eighty-three became the most articulate witness of the morning.

"Faye wanted them Dunlap acres connecting Corbitt land deeded to Prin. He won them fair from her daddy, but he always felt guilty, winning the parcel from Corbitt at cards and all. He'd of signed them over to Joyce before she died if she ever give him the time a day." Amos paused to cough into a handkerchief so white it snapped. "So when him and Prin got together, he naturally done what he aimed to do for forty years. But you know how he was for saving, and he wrote them instructions on the tag end of his will."

Judge Harlan sighed. "J. R. and Billy Todd say that ain't Faye's writing."

"When would they of studied old Faye's handwriting? They never got far enough out of town to get a letter. Big Bill'd be the one to ask if he wasn't dead."

The judged sighed again. Everyone in town knew that William Custer Dunlap's name had been chipped eight feet up on the Vietnam Memorial and that old Faye had climbed a ladder himself to make the rubbing that hung on his living room wall.

"I suppose you're right, Amos," he said before he called George Samuels from the bank, who agreed that the signature was Faye's, then Doc Wilson, who said it wasn't.

Finally, he looked out at the two men and their lawyer and at Carlotta's grandmother with her lawyer. "Anything else?"

Neither lawyer jumped to his feet, and the judge mouthed, "The court will take ten minutes," while he banged the gavel across his words.

A few people stood to flex their arms, but most stayed put until the judge returned and cracked his wooden hammer on the wooden desk again.

"Since nobody can concur on whether old Faye wrote that note himself before he died, I guess it's up to me to decide."

He glowered at the courtroom. "And I don't want a disturbance about what I say. I know some of you can get hot-headed at times." He may have been referring to the occasion a few years earlier when J.R. drowned half a dozen spur-fitted roosters in a stock tank after their owner accused him of fixing the cockfight. "I'll throw the book at anybody making threats or doing any kind of devilment—since I got to rule in favor of Princess Lynn Corbitt Wagner Bates Dunlap." He charged on before anyone snickered, which often happened when someone read out Prin's string of legal names, the first of which Joyce Corbitt had chosen from the label of a maternity dress. "I'm awarding them acres to the entitled widow whether or not Faye wrote that note. You boys keep the pasture land and the house." He repounded the mallet. "Court's adjourned."

Carlotta unwound and stood up, towering over the dainty woman's dandelion hair. "All right, Granny, let's go."

Three

"Not that I think she did spoon arsenic over his eggs," Carlotta said to the horse as she cinched the saddle. "But she's sure fire capable."

She adjusted the bridle on the nose too blunt to qualify as Arabian even though a Middle Eastern strain constituted half the gene pool, and put her foot in the stirrup. "Oh, hell." She halted in mid-swing. "There's liable to be March snakes out."

She dropped to the ground, latched the reins around a fence post, and loped to the house.

As she flung open the door, her grandmother came into the kitchen. "I thought you left already."

"I forgot the pistol. After Smokey got bit by that blind rattler, I ain't taking any chances."

"Don't shoot yourself in the foot."

"You say that every time." She took the gun from the top of the refrigerator and shook a few shells from the box into her palm.

Prin ignored her and opened the refrigerator door festooned with plastic oreo magnets. "Shit. We're out of pound cake."

"Cake's fattening." Carlotta clicked the safety catch.

"It don't seem to blimp you out."

"I'm thirty years younger than you, Granny."

"And still a spinster. I had your mama when I was fifteen, and your mama had you—"

"—when she was fifteen." Carlotta slammed the kitchen door on the words and strode across the yard while she tucked the pistol in the pocket of her jean jacket. She opened her eyes wide and mimicked for the horse, "'And you never had a date yet.'"

She climbed into the saddle, touched the horse's sides with her heels, and they cantered down the dirt road. She paused almost at once to climb off and unfasten the barbed wire loop that held the gate shut. But rather than laying the posts carefully in the weeds as she usually did, she kicked the gate into a tangle of wood and wire. "It's Granny's land now, so I guess we don't need a fence, do we?"

She remounted and turned the not-quite-Arabian head uphill.

The horse picked its way through the brittle milkweed and fesque to the edge of the cedar woods while Carlotta watched for rattlers. "Snakes don't care to fang you and use up a month's worth of venom when they can't swallow you whole, but if they don't see you coming, they get spooked."

"Ain't that a sign you're losing your mind? Talking to yourself?"

Her knees clamped the saddle and her head jerked alert.

Billy Todd Dunlap hunkered on a limestone outcropping and stared down at her with eyes the blue of ripe juniper berries.

"I was talking to Blaze."

"Same thing," he said. "You out inspecting your new land?"

Her chin came up. "It's Granny's land. I ain't involved."

He slid off the ledge of rock. "It's a damned nice piece."

"It ain't got squat to do with me."

He reached out to stroke the horse's neck, and although his arm brushed her knee, he didn't seem to notice. "I bet you never seen a view like it's got from back there."

Her lips stiffened. "I don't bet."

He laughed. "I didn't mean literally, lunkhead." He tugged the lead from her fingers. "Come on. I'll show you. Blaze can stay here if you can walk in them untied shoes."

She jumped down while he strung the reins around a sapling. "I can walk in them." Her eyes swept his jeans. "At least you ain't fat like J.R."

"Nobody's fat like J.R." He gestured beyond the jut of stone. "That way."

"Hell, I don't know where we're supposed to be going. You lead."

"You sure are mouthy to your elders, ain't you?"

She snorted. "You're two years older than me."

"Three."

Their feet snapped dead juniper needlets, kicked up stone chips. Once he swung aside a cedar branch that might have slapped her cheek if he hadn't held it.

"How far is this fabulous view?"

"Up by the bluff." He glanced over his shoulder. "Your granny got a heap of good looking land this morning." When she stopped, he put his hand on her arm. "Hey, I was just joshing you. Come on."

She stiffened, but followed him. "Well, knock off that guilt-tripping crap then."

A minute later, his fingers fell from her sleeve to rest on her hand. "Walk this way."

"This better be good."

In another few minutes, they came through the trees onto the panorama of a meadow, the slash of a blue-white river, and a valley ringed by wine-colored mountains. Masses of aching yellow jonquils bordered the bowl-sides of the meadow.

Carlotta caught her breath. "Well, I'll be damned. That *is* some view."

He took her hand again and pulled her with him to the ground. "Sit here on this flat rock. It's even better."

They sat a moment in silence while two hawks glided across the cloudless sky, their dual shadows black wingspans on the meadow floor.

"How come you got the name Carlotta?"

"Not everybody's got a dead war hero brother to be named after."

"Hey, I just wondered."

She studied him, then shrugged. "When I was born, Granny thought I'd grow a head of black hair, but the black wore off and came in dishwater blonde."

"It ain't a bad color."

Then he stood up and looked down soberly at her for a few seconds before he turned and started back the way they'd come.

Four

That evening the phone rang half a dozen times, but each time Prin reached it, only deliberate silence came across the line.

Her query, "Who is this?" progressed to "Who you want to talk to?" to "Who the hell do you think you're dealing with?" to finally, "We're shutting off the damned bell."

"You think it's J.R., Granny?"

"Or that piss-ant Billy Todd." She fumbled with the telephone. "I could tell they was both mad as hornets this morning."

"I didn't think Billy Todd cared much."

"What would you know? The Dunlaps never could abide losing. Especially when land's at stake."

Carlotta scooted forward on the sewing rocker and stood up. "I'm going to bed."

Prin smoothed her stiff yellow hair. "Shut off that caterwauling TV on your way. This phone crap's got me too nervous to watch."

Carlotta kicked her bedroom door shut and pulled off her jacket. When the pistol banged her hip, she took it from the jacket pocket and placed it on the nightstand table beside a brass lamp.

The gun barrel and the lamp base reflected filaments of light, and she snapped off the lamp before she removed her shirt and pulled on checkered cotton pajamas. She stood and looked out onto the dirt yard that lay almost white in the moonlight.

Finally, she turned back the bed quilt and stretched out to stare at the ceiling across which the moon trailed a rope of light.

She closed her eyes to the sound of her grandmother in the kitchen rummaging in a drawer.

She opened them again to complete darkness.

A rasp of labored breathing filled the room, and the dark silhouette of a man blocked the window rectangle.

She sat up. "What?"

The rustle of jean material across a windowsill came just before the thud of boots hit the ground. The silhouette disappeared.

"Is that you, Billy Todd?"

As she flung aside the covers, her hand came down on the night table and the pistol. She swept up the gun, sprang to the window, and threw herself feet first outside.

The moon no longer lit the yard, and the man, his shape indistinguishable, merged with the cedars. She sprinted after him, the revolver tallow-smooth in her fist.

"Billy Todd!"

Her bare feet snapped twigs as she raced toward the woods, her breath puffed mist into the air, and the thrash of someone running came from ahead.

She gained the tree line, but didn't slow her run.

Nor did she pause to aim in the darkness as she raised the gun toward the boot sounds and pulled the trigger.

The crack of the shot bounded and rebounded against the black trees.

What might have been a scream shrilled upward, and the sound echoed into widening circles of black nothingness.

She stopped abruptly. "You stupid fool! It's only land!"

Now only silence surrounded the clouds that shifted to reveal a white moon caught motionless in the ribs of a dead cedar, and the stillness obscured the cry that might have been meant for the man or for herself as she hurled the pistol as hard as she could into the black underbrush.

"You stupid fool! It's a fucking piece of land!"

A NIGHT IN THE PORT AUTHORITY

"We arrive at the New York Port Authority Bus Terminal in ten minutes." The driver's announcement crackles over the speaker into the cold air. "All passengers change here, so remove your belongings from the bus."

I watch midnight lights through the tinted bus-window glass and hard rain. The red traffic signals, blue neon, the lavender mercury vapor flicker in the downpour as the bus speeds along the night streets and reduces the city to window height.

The bus lurches around a dark corner, slows for a tunnel entrance, then bursts into the glare of an underground garage. The brakes wheeze to a jolting stop in a line of buses.

"New York Port Authority."

I grab my weekender and shoulder bag and reach the curb before the other passengers untangle their suitcases and cardboard cartons from the overhead racks.

"Where do I get the connecting bus to Saratoga Springs?" I feel in the shoulder bag for the paperback copy of *Middlemarch* where my ticket is securely tucked.

"Check at the Adirondack counter. Upstairs."

I hurry into the waiting room and zigzag through the crowd toward the escalator. As I pass the bolted rows of chairs, I sense that every seat is taken.

I glide up from the packed waiting room to the upper lobby—which is completely empty.

No chairs have been anchored to this floor, and I step off into a shrouded corridor of polished white marble lined with ticket counters and shop fronts. But the alcoves of the bus lines, lunchrooms, and boutiques are covered with iron screening. Only nightlights illuminate the logos, and *Greyhound, Chock-Full-O-Nuts, Northeast*, all of which face the escalator, are padlocked behind the sturdy iron webbing. The people who've ridden upstairs with me are heading briskly toward the glass street doors that open to the rain and spraying traffic.

The only occupant of the lobby is a surly-jawed janitor pushing an auditorium broom. He doesn't look up, and I have the uneasy sensation that my loafer heels are tapping along a shuttered street in the middle of the night. My pulse quickens with my pace.

Then, halfway down the deserted hallway, I see the stylized green mountains, the stylized neon script spelling *Adirondack*, and the comforting reflection of fluorescence on a uniformed clerk.

"What time does the bus leave for Saratoga Springs?" With an exhalation of relief I place the ticket envelope on the white counter sheen.

"6:25." No twitch of eyelid or muscle acknowledges the ticket.

"What time?"

"6:25 a.m."

"I meant the *next* one."

"That's the next one." He's gazing past my shoulder, and I turn my head to see another attendant in an identical uniform loosening the accordion-pleated iron mesh. Both men wear caps with plastic rain covers.

"Six a.m. is *six hours* from now."

Neither man bothers to nod. Nor does the one under the logo deign to shrug as he rounds the counter. "We have to close now. We open at six in the morning."

"I can exchange this ticket for one to Albany. I can get a taxi from there to Saratoga. It's just that I don't like to fly, and I took the bus from New Orleans so I— " I hear the strands of alarm in my voice.

The man wielding the iron chain gate favors me with mild kindness as he scoops the ticket envelope from the counter and wedges it beneath my hand. "No bus leaves the Port Authority for any destination until six in the morning."

My shock allows them to move me aside, and it takes a few seconds for me to say, "I can't believe that in the city of New York everything closes down like—" I watch helplessly as they padlock the chain links in place. "What am I supposed to do until—?"

"We open at six."

They walk toward the street door without a backward glance.

The fluorescent lights of the counter have been extinguished, and the hands of a moon clock face, the only bright disc of light on the wall, click to 12:35.

It's too late to walk the streets and find a hotel room even if it weren't raining. It's almost too late to hail a cab.

I decide the best thing to do is go back downstairs.

At least in the lower brightly lit room, there are chairs and the presence of other stranded passengers whose compulsory company can dispel the ominous gloom of the vacant marble hallway.

I'm tempted to run to the escalator.

But I don't. I restrain myself to an accelerated walk and try not to hear the echo of my own footsteps as I finally reach for the handrail of the descending stairs.

The handrail and the stairs are no longer moving.

The escalator has been turned off with the upstairs lights.

I stumble down the motionless, uneven steps to the lower floor that's fortunately still brightly lit and still jammed with people. And I see that every seat in the rows of chairs is indeed taken.

Beyond the chairs, people hunch on the floor and lean against the wainscoting—both of white ceramic tile rather than marble—with their chins on their chests and their eyes closed. A woman in a sleeveless flower print dress under a mat of Spanish-moss hair is sponge bathing in the alabaster drinking fountain.

As I pass her, muttering to herself as she diligently wets her fingertips and scrubs her elbow, a disquieting insight makes me look closely at the resigned lobby people, at their unraveling cuffs and broken shoes.

None of them will be leaving in six hours. Nor in six days.

I've climbed off the bus into an immobile circle of the dispossessed.

That awareness is numbing, and I head toward the scarred door marked *LAD ES*, with the vague notion that the restroom might contain a couch or possibly an attendant who will make eye contact in return for a tip.

But the room contains nothing but metal stalls with doors askew, a waste bin overflowing with used paper toweling, and half a dozen stained washbasins. It's uncannily silent after the subdued exhaling, muffled trembling and snuffling from the homeless outside the door, and I stand a moment before the mirror that reflects my sagging shoulders.

The reflection of a black girl with brass ear loops and a jean jacket appears in the glass behind me. "I'd get out of here if I was you, girl. There was a rape in here just last night."

Adrenaline thuds into my temples. I grab the shoulder bag and weekender and fling myself into the lobby.

The girl has already disappeared.

I sway against the wall and press my head into the ceramic tiles while I control my breathing.

Over five hours to go.

An old man, with eyes and a knitted cap of the same faded blue, wobbles slowly through the lobby, supporting himself with a cheap cane and bumping a gray string sack against his knees. His grizzled skin has eroded into vertical crevices that no longer define jowls or a neck, and his back humps into the curvature of a pigeon's breast.

The old man falters toward the exit doors where buses wait unattended, and I notice a much younger man on a rolled sleeping bag watching him. The young man, in a crumpled work shirt, faded khaki pants, and wing-tips with no socks, sits on the bedroll with his fingers tipping a vacant globe and his bare ankles jutting from the dress shoes in nearly the same brown as the leather. He doesn't move as his dark eyes, shaded by a yachting cap, rest with pity on the ancient white man.

I nudge the weekender with my foot, bracing it against the wall to use as a seat.

But the overnight case is a modest cube whose top handle makes comfort impossible, and I last only a few seconds before I ease off onto the floor.

The tiles are icy through my jeans, but I sit until the old man disappears out an exit door. Then I adjust the strap of my shoulder bag and stand up again.

The young man on the sleeping bag is the only person in this Cimmerian underworld whose face has registered sympathy. He's the only one here whose eyes have actually looked at someone else. And his sleeping bag is large enough for two.

But I don't know the rules for striking up an acquaintance with a New York street black in such an absurd night cavern. He glanced with compassion at an old white man, but since I'm not an old white man, how will he react if I approach him?

I noticed him, but he may not want to be noticed— and if the sympathy of his gazing at the old man was involuntary, he may prefer not to notice anyone else.

What if I go over and speak, and he rebuffs my attempt at conversation?

As I study him from my wall, he leans forward and clasps his hands together, and I'm jolted with uneasiness. What if someone else has observed his kindness and goes up to him before I do? I could never approach two young blacks.

With no notion what I'll say, I find myself reaching for the overnight case and walking across the lobby. I stop at the wing tips, and he looks up.

"Is there room on that for two of us?" I indicate the sleeping bag, amazed at how calm I sound. "All the other seats in here seem to be taken."

He grins and scoots to one end of the bag. "This place like this every night. Maybe some worse in the rain, but not much."

I sit carefully, not too close, aligning the weekender at the rim of the bedroll for an armrest so I can reasonably incline away from his shoulder. I'm sure young black guys have set stereotypes about white women, and I try to think of a bland comment. But as my gaze accidentally meets his, I blurt, "Are you one of the homeless, too?"

Jesus, I think.

Fortunately he gives me another grin. "Naw. I drive cars over for a dealer in Chicago. Four hundred bucks and a bus ticket home." He swings a rose-hued palm in an arc that embraces the lobby. "Don't nothing move out a here until morning."

"I noticed."

"But, hey, them peoples don't care. They ain't going nowhere."

We sit a moment looking at the limp grayness of the crowd, and he shifts the yachting cap. "Ain't this place the pit, though? See that girl over there? With the earrings?" He jabs his chin toward a girl with exaggerated ribbons of rhinestones dangling to her bare shoulders. Her summer smock is too flimsy for the air conditioning and too tight to accommodate her swollen uterus. "She one a the regulars down here. Soon as she start showing, her pimp throw her out. She don't bother with tricks now, just cadges enough for cigarettes, a line a coke once in a while, maybe some horse. Just down here waiting for the baby to come."

"That's awful!"

He nods.

I've relaxed. "You know, sometimes I think—"

Three policemen swing through the exit doors and stride in step, their black belts, straps, holsters, and hat bills in gleaming patent leather, black nightsticks, crisp blue shirts and corded twill trousers. They glitter with determination, silver badges and buckles, as they march to the bolted seats and crack the chair backs with their sticks.

"Move along there. You can't sleep in here. Move along."

The sleepers stagger groggily erect, stumble to the wall until the police pass. Then they resettle in the seats like a disturbed and returning flock of birds.

At the end of the room, the policemen stop beside a thin black teen asleep with his head in the lap of an emaciated blond girl.

"Get up there. You can't sleep it off in here."

"Leave him alone." The girl throws a pale arm across him.

One of the officers pokes him with his baton. "We ought to take him outside and sober him up." He lifts the kid by one tee-shirted shoulder, and though the boy's face twists in pain, he doesn't open his eyes.

"Don't get involved," the young man beside me warns in a low voice. It's as if he's detected some movement I didn't know I'd made. "Won't do no good, and could get everybody in worse trouble."

A fourth policeman reaches the group before I've realized that another one has come in. "We got a call," he says. "Let's go."

The one wringing the teen's shoulder says, "He's stoned."

"Everybody's stoned. Let's go."

The cop opens his fist, and the boy pitches into the girl's skirt. She leans across him protectively.

The four officers swing in an unwavering file out the doors and are gone.

I realize I've been holding my breath. "Damn." I swallow. "They seemed about seven feet tall."

The young man adjusts his cap. "Maybe eight."

I smile at him while I catch sight of a young white man descending the stalled escalator, an athlete in a white school sweater with orange initials, *UC*, on the pocket. His carrot-colored hair and freckled innocence match the fuzzy letters as he weaves toward a section of unoccupied wall, slumps into a long-legged bundle, and drops his glassy stare onto his knees.

"About what a college degree be worth to some them kids out there," my companion observes.

And we lean against the wall and talk about the state of education, about children, discipline and the proliferation of praise and prize-giving that's robbing American kids of anticipation and motivation. I let myself use my normal stock of words, and I'm amazed at how comfortable, how natural, the conversation feels.

During one of the comfortable pauses, I offer, "If we can find an all-night place around here that serves coffee, I owe you a cup for the loan of your sleeping bag."

"They got a twenty-four hour coffee shop down the street a couple a blocks."

"I'll risk the rain if you will."

He unflexes, retrieves my case and his sleeping bag. "I could use a cup."

We go upstairs and out into the rain that's become crystals sparkling from streetlights and headlights, not falling but slanting into our faces with the fine spume of a ferry. Cars splash by, and we run against a red light to shelter under a construction scaffolding.

"This way."

But abruptly, uneasiness gathers in my chest.

No other pedestrians sprint down the street, which is deserted and dark, and I'm certain no taxi is about to stop. What if he isn't leading me to a coffee shop after all? I suggested going for coffee, but what if—

Before the thought forms fully, I see ahead a slash of red neon and a lighted window.

"Who-o-e-e," he says as we spring inside the tiny café that reeks of stale smoke, grease, and burnt eggs.

We shake off the mist, but rain has soaked our clothes and hair and we exude an odor of wet fur.

"What do you take in your coffee?" I ask over my shoulder as I approach the counter.

"The works."

"Me, too." I pay, collect two brown crockery mugs, sugar, and powdered cream packets before I join him at a miniature table to drink the doctored, coffee-flavored water.

But it's hot, and we accept a refill from the groggy waitress.

A glass cake stand on the counter holds glaze-crackled donuts, and I feel myself getting lightheaded with caffeine and hunger. But I can't come up with the right phrase that can offer to buy us something to eat, so we finish the last of our coffee and leave the trolley-sized restaurant.

The walk back seems shorter with the rain behind us, but we're still thoroughly damp by the time we plunge into the darkened upper lobby.

The pregnant girl with the earrings is huddled in a window ledge, her arms crossed for warmth over her great belly. A dwarf, doubled into the window with her, inhales a hand-rolled cigarette and passes it to her. I walk by them with the sensation that I've seen them in the Port Authority countless times.

I follow my companion downstairs, he replaces the sleeping bag on the floor, plants the weekender at one end, and we sit down again.

The cavernous room is colder than it was earlier.

This time I bring up politics, and I'm not surprised that we belong to the same party or that we agree on what the country needs. I watch his alert brown eyes and the dark-ridged tendons of his hands as he describes the crumbling blocks he drives through on his auto deliveries, and we spend a lot of time talking about the unemployed and the homeless.

"All them throwaway peoples," he says morosely. "You think things be better one a these days, but it don't seem like." He shrugs and nods at the fat copy of *Middlemarch* protruding from my shoulder bag. "You read a lot?"

"All the time."

"I thought so." He nods again. "My wife, she like to read, too."

It's his first reference to the personal, but before I can follow up, he adds, "Almost morning out there."

"Are you sure?" I glance around, but everything looks exactly as it has all night. No one in the room changes position. No one is stirring. "What time do you think it is?"

He grins. "About six."

He doesn't wear a watch, and I look at him. "Are you sure?"

He nods once more. "What time your bus leaving?"

"Six twenty-five."

"What line?"

"Adirondack."

He tugs at his cap brim and points with his chin. "Last door down there." He unlimbers and stands up. "I got a later bus."

It's my cue to stand as he shoulders the bedroll and takes up my weekender.

"Hey, thanks for sharing your sleeping bag." We're walking toward the door at the far end, the only people in the lobby who are moving.

"No sweat."

We arrive at the door, and outside waits a bus whose lighted slot reads *Albany-Saratoga Springs*. Standing beside the open bus door is—miraculously, as if he's materialized without having existed until that moment—a uniformed driver.

The young man drops the sleeping bag and extends his hand. "Kennedy."

Although the hand feels as bony as it looks, it's also very warm and firm. "Walker," I say.

I want to articulate the important, the perceptive thing that will summarize our brief acquaintance, our companionship, and our agreement so he'll understand what I'm feeling and I'll know he knows, but I can't think of that significant, illuminating thing, and I don't say anything.

"Have a good trip." He hands me the weekender.

"You, too."

And because that's an exit line, I go through the glass door he holds open for me. It flows shut behind me.

I hold out the now foreign envelope with the ticket to Saratoga Springs, and the driver takes it without a grimace or an apology or an acknowledgement of how things have altered in the last six hours.

I glance at the exit door as I climb the bus steps, and the young man behind the glass tips his yachting cap.

I lift my hand in a salute.

I sit down in the first row and shove my case under the seat. But when I look through the tinted window again, the doorway to the lobby is empty.

The bus is iced as if the air-conditioner has stayed on all night.

DOWNWARD TO DARKNESS

One

"See there. You're fixing to balance steady on your hooves again." She urged the gelding onto ropy legs, talking him upright. "You ain't about to let a tumble and meager thump on the head jar you into a concussion."

She caressed the little horse, reassuring his wavering eyes, and when a motor keened down the hill, she merely glanced at the approaching pick-up without interrupting her soothing incantation.

The woman driving the red pick-up gunned to a ferocious idle and electronically rolled down the window. She seemed unaware of the woman-to-horse monologue in the yard as she said, "Do you know anyone around who could look at my engine, Min? I think it has problems. Oh, what a sweet pony."

Min shoved at her cropped bangs. "'Sweet' ain't quite the word I'd bestow on him." She spoke with the exaggerated drawl she used around the vice president whose bank carpets she vacuumed after closing. "I guess nobody knows cars better than my son-in-law Burns." Her gaze swept the obviously new truck bed. "He owns the garage on Highway 16 just after you top the bridge."

"Oh, how wonderful!"

Min had already told Burns about the woman who'd rented her house nestled in the cedars. "She obviously dyes her hair blue-black, and she raves on and on, magnifying the fall leaf colors, praising the bathroom faucets like they couldn't be bought any weekday at Lowe's."

Burns had looked up from his book at the kitchen table. "I hope you got a month's rent in advance. No city gal's likely to fire up that wood stove more than once."

"She forked over first and last without a blink."

"Good for you, Min." He'd laughed as his eyes returned to the book.

Min's gaze veered to the scarlet lips in the scarlet pick-up window. "You want to come in and use the phone?" Her hand gentled the pony's neck. "Burns keeps a tow truck."

"I think I can make it." She smiled the varnished smile Min had also described. "Wish me luck." Her red nails flickered a wave.

Min dutifully nodded as the red tailgate accelerated through the stream intersecting the county road.

"Bouncing a toy truck across hubcap-high water is as good a way as any to render your brakes dead useless, ain't it, Jack? You notice how them wire-hard curls make you mindful of Nolda?"

She concentrated on the horse, but it was only a matter of seconds before she braced her jaw and lifted her gaze toward the trailer clinging to the top of the hill. Fall oak leaves had shriveled tidily along the ridge, and the trailer now glared bone white against the cedars.

"Looks exactly the same as when Stu first hauled it up there to live with Nolda in front of my eyes, don't it?"

The horse nudged her, and she again met the water-colored eyes whose lemony lashes disappeared unless the sun shone behind them. "You're right. I got no call to be studying that trailer." Her fingers furrowed his mane. "It's the sorry truth, but you don't look a thing like your daddy. If I'd guessed you'd end up so washed out, I'd of waited and sold you instead of Big Jack, you know that, don't you?"

She stared between his pallid ears as if she re-saw the half-ton truck with stock panels carrying Big Jack away through the creek ford.

"Who'd of guessed seeing that horse trucked off was worse than seeing Stu Hammond walk out of that courtroom a free man?"

The pony's crooked nose bobbed and his lips curled back from square yellow teeth as if, of course, he knew.

Two

She centered a plate of fried chicken on the laminated placemat and stepped to the kitchen doorway. "Supper's ready, boys."

"This is a rerun of *Law and Order* I ain't seen, Grandma." Chesley sank deeper into the Lazy-Boy.

Wesley shifted on the braided rug and smiled up at her. "Me neither."

She didn't say that he wouldn't know if he'd watched it the hour before. She merely produced a bemused smile.

She and Deborah and Burns had manufactured the illusion that Chesley excelled at books but that Wesley would eventually be good with his hands. Chesley accepted the fiction, but he'd told her that the eighth grade teacher—"Sorry as she is, Grandma"—did know that Wesley couldn't tell one alphabet letter from another or a 10 from a 6. Chesley said the school kept them in class together only because Wesley collapsed in terror when he was separated from his twin.

She watched them a moment. "I can pour this platter out for George if you boys don't want it."

George lifted his head from the linoleum and looked at her without anticipation.

"You won't risk chicken bones on a pedigree collie, Grandma," Chesley said with good-natured flatness as he stared serenely at the TV screen.

"Well, suit yourselves." She returned to the stove to wipe frying grease from the burners. "But cold gravy on colder mashed potatoes ain't what I'd elect to eat if I could dish up everything nice and hot."

Chesley called, "The commercial's about to come on."

She told Burns Chesley was the exact image of him at thirteen, "—except for his eyes being near black rather than green."

The first time she'd looked down into Burns' vivid, almost chartreuse, stare had been nearly two years after she and Stu had adopted Nolda. "You're a true Christian, Min, taking in that orphan girl, and now your late cousin's boy." That's what they all said, and she answered coolly, "Well, there's nobody else, and with me and Stu having only Deborah, it don't seem right to give them two up to foster care." But the truth was, she'd begged for them both. Dainty, beautiful Nolda, so kind to Deborah, and Burns, little as he was, examining the hills, books, shattered clocks or electric razors with the same back-lit intensity. "It's a quality you can't put a finger on," she'd said to Stu. "Like a scoop of mist off the morning river or a—" But Stu regarded her strangely and she'd stopped.

Stu, of course, had been the one to suggest driving Burns to the dump so he could retrieve broken objects with intriguing mangled parts, and Stu said Burns reveled in the trash as if he'd wandered into a toyshop.

And back home while he unloaded his cartons, his eyes green as hickory hulls, he held up a cracked radio. "They had the negative and positive turned around." Or a discarded drill. "If they had the sense to scrape off the rust, this would work in no time." And he'd shake his head. "No wonder garbage is fixing to take over the world."

His teachers confided they could never challenge him enough, and they encouraged her and Stu to send him to the community college when he graduated.

But that had been before Stu and Nolda ran away together.

She jockeyed the chicken grease into a coffee can. "Chesley, I'm aiming to put this food away."

The twins fumbled into the kitchen, and she watched Chesley ladle up potatoes molded to a spoon curve.

"Didn't I say they'd be cold as mud in a spring ditch?" she said while Chesley reached for the gravy, cooled to the consistency of school paste.

He laid a chicken breast on Wesley's plate, a thigh on his own. "Is this your great peach cobbler, Grandma?"

"Peach cobbler would be better hot, too."

"Your cobbler's good any way at all, Grandma." He grinned at her.

"Go on now and finish your show while I clean up this filthy kitchen."

"You never had a filthy kitchen in your life," Chesley said as they jostled through the door into the living room.

Min glanced out the kitchen window as the red pick-up sped by in the dusk, taking the grade too fast.

"I guess she stopped for Burns to look at her motor," she said to the glass.

"What, Grandma?"

"Nothing."

As she turned from the darkening view, the headlights of Burns' ancient truck barreled toward the upper pasture where his and Stu's cattle grazed.

Burns had told her, reluctantly, that he was keeping half his herd on the top with Stu's, and she'd nodded. "It's all right with me as long as you shut the gate so Stu Hammond's cows don't crop my pasture. But you warn him I'll shoot on sight any animal of his in my field. I don't care if it's a newborn calf or that fancy persimmon-colored bull he's so proud of. If it's on my land, it'll be strip sirloin for the buzzards."

Burns had studied her. "It's been fifteen years since the divorce."

"Seventeen."

"And you got everything you asked for from Judge Perkins."

"Stu Hammond's sorry luck in court that day wasn't my doing. People around here don't cotton to fathers running off with daughters, and I figure Linwood

Perkins knew what he was about when he parceled me the bottom land and gave Stu that scrub oak along the hillside."

"Nolda and Stu aren't related, Min."

"I never made you nor Deborah nor the twins choose sides, did I?"

Nor did she remind him that Stu's flight had cost him the community college.

She looked down from the dark window, stared grimly into the sink, and without scouring the enamel, turned on the water to swirl the unused cleanser down the drain. "Well, with all the rest, what's another helping of waste in the world?" she asked too softly to be heard over the television.

Three

The next afternoon she watched the black-haired woman descend the hill, walking this time, her laced blue boots—the vivid blue shade of the highlights in her black hair—avoiding the muddiest ruts.

"I want to thank you for sending me to your son-in-law's garage." She wore a raspberry-red sweater the shade of her lipstick and nails.

"He's good with machines."

The glittering smile beamed past Min toward the pond. "Are those wild ducks?"

"Mallards. But I hatched them from eggs."

"How beautiful!" She took a step in their direction. "But will they be all right in the winter if they don't fly south?"

"Maybe they think this *is* the south," Min said dryly.

"Oh, Min, I'll have to use that." And she added ebulliently, "This is such a wonderful place to write!"

Min merely looked at her, but before the silence expanded, George loped around the house and Min could grab his collar. "Don't go jumping on Mrs. Endicott now."

"What a sweet collie!" She touched his regal nose. "But it hasn't been 'Mrs.' for a long time." She glanced at Min. "And I'd rather be called 'Teal.' It's a color of blue."

Min nodded. She'd read the signature on the rent check aloud to Burns and had said, "Why would anybody name a kid a color of blue?" But now she merely said, "I guess I never heard of 'Teal' as a name."

"My mother loved decorator books. When she went into the hospital to have me, she had a copy of *Better Homes and Gardens* with her, and when I was born, she said, 'Teal.' My father was convinced it was the shade of paint she wanted for the nursery, but the obstetrics staff beaded it on a bracelet to snap around my wrist, so it became my name."

She paused for a response, and after a moment Min drawled, "When Deborah, that's my daughter, birthed the twins, the hospital put the name bands on opposite, so the baby Burns intended as 'Wesley' was 'Chesley' and 'Chesley' was 'Wesley.'"

"That's your son-in-law, Burns Rutledge, who owns the garage?"

A cerise nail plucked carelessly at a loop of raspberry wool around the too-casual intonation of his name.

Min glanced sharply toward her. "Yes, that's my son-in-law," she said dryly.

Four

She balanced the shotgun to ascertain that the safety held.

"A man can't help but be flattered by a woman repeating his name like it was embroidered in lavender yarn. Especially a man like Burns, marrying so young and all."

A hawk sailed overhead, sliding a black shadow along the pasture.

"Deborah won't insist, Min, but I want to do what's right," he'd said, and she'd finally murmured, "I guess it ain't fair to saddle twins with a blank space on their birth certificates where the father's name is aimed to go." And he'd agreed to the marriage because she'd said so.

"By rights, Deborah should be the one nettled by that woman. But she don't have a feel for enviousness." She watched the hawk circle. "Deborah would take such female conniving just as mournful as she takes everything else. Admitting at fifteen she was as much to blame as him, knowing full well if they hadn't been living in the same house, a boy like Burns would never give her a second look."

She reached the gate where hot-pink daubing on the tree bark alerted hunters that the land was posted.

"It's a crying shame they ain't a paint to warn away man-hunters," she said while she lowered the rifle barrel toward a weed beside the road.

Five

"I guess I don't rightly appreciate winter," she said to the dog. "It's too snug a time for temptation." She pressed the screen door open with her grocery sack and George trotted in. "Even Stu and Nolda run off right before Christmas."

The window gleamed a polished night mirror, and she stared at her night reflection. Burns had told her once that glass only appeared stationary while it actually crawled in constant motion toward the sill. "In a few thousand years, there won't be a pane but only glass molecules piled along the sash," he'd said.

Now she looked at the dog. "Is that the way with me and you, George? Both of us slithering down to nothing but a puddle of molecules?"

She unstacked hamburger, hot-dogs, buns. "I don't recall the last time I run into Stu. Nolda I caught sight of at Walmart's maybe a year back, but I near didn't recognize her. As a little bit of a thing, she was always whipping around, curls flying, eyes as blue as ripe juniper berries. But there in the dry beans aisle, she shuffled along, sullied out, her hair grayer than mine."

George tilted his head into a listening position.

"But I guess what matters is that neither of us ever in our lives had the money to pair a sweater to a tube of cherry lipstick and a bottle of cherry nail polish."

Six

"Come on, Wesley, I'll saddle Cinnamon so you can ride." Chesley tightened the cinch on Jack.

"Naw." Wesley dropped to the yellow grass. "I'll stay here with Grandma."

Min laid her hand on his hair. "You go on, Chesley. You know he don't like horses."

"I thought he could at least learn to do something."

But his defensive sulk was interrupted by Burns' truck crossing the creek, cutting through the crystal sheaves of water.

The boys called it his yellow truck, but 'yellow' was only a convenience since both fenders had been replaced—one in faded lime, the other in discontinued gray—a brown tailgate, unearthed from an auto graveyard, had been substituted for the original, and the metal skin of the lemon-colored hood festered with maroon rust.

As Burns paused beside them, Min glanced pointedly at the stock panels attached to the truck bed. "You aiming to move some cattle?"

Burns had creamy, untannable skin—"Not wormy looking but more like the good white oak of prize egg baskets," she'd said once—and now he pushed dark hair back from a pale forehead. "I hear they're paying top dollar at the livestock auction." He didn't meet her gaze. "I thought I'd take C.E. Faber a couple of bull calves."

Min watched his fingers twitch as he shifted gears. "C.E. Faber buys beef for dog food. You ain't getting top dollar from him."

But the truck lunged forward across her words, churning new corrugations in the road, and she stared at the cab's rear window, banded across by two rifles in the gun rack.

"It ain't like your daddy to be selling in winter when cattle weights is off."

Chesley swung onto the pony. "Grandpa has cancer." He clamped his heels to the little horse's sides, and Jack sprang away.

"What does that mean, Grandma?" Wesley blinked after him.

"So Stu Hammond has cancer."

"Is Grandpa going to die?"

"Everybody's going to die one time or another."

Then she looked at him, crouched beside her, and added in a soothing command, "Now you go fetch a brick and a hammer and we'll crack some black walnuts for fudge."

"Watch me, Grandma!" Wesley cried, immediately reassured. "I'll whack them shells to smithereens."

Seven

She stared down at the sweater Stu had bought himself one birthday. He'd joked that the present he never wanted was a parrot that could live a hundred years and persist after he was dead and buried. And now as she pulled her arm through the cashmere-blend sleeve, she murmured, "But here you are, Stu Hammond, being outlasted by a button-up coat sweater."

She took a jacket and stocking cap from their nails and layered them on, located her faded garage-sale mittens, flashlight, and halter. "When that fool horse didn't come in for his six o'clock feed, I reckoned I'd be obliged to go look for him."

Night obscured the snowfall, but the instant she stepped out, sleet pocked her cheekbones, and when she clicked on the flashlight, snowflakes streamed toward the bulb in white strings.

She zipped the jacket higher, firmed her lips, and tottered up the hill.

She went through the gate and sprayed the light beam toward the tree line. The weak disk of illumination flattened against the snow as she rounded the bend in the road that led to the rent house. Although she flung the feeble light ahead, the snow, as thick as dangling bolts of lace, revealed nothing.

"Well, I guess it won't hurt Jack to stay the night up here. Teal Endicott ain't home anyways."

But then a sudden odor of wood smoke filtered through the snow.

She inhaled the frightening scent of burning wood, perhaps tongue-in-groove slats browning, over-heated, ready to catch. She hurried forward, looking hard for the house, until at last a dark mass rose behind the snow.

But instead of a snow-laden porch, the flashlight beam hit the brown tailgate of a once-yellow Ford.

She sucked in a mouthful of snow, spun around, and spooled the torch into a careening arch as she stumbled down the frozen road and snapped it off. "Damn her, damn her," she panted. "God damn her."

Eight

The white sky crumbled around her in great consolidated flakes.

"As soon as I spotted them red talons, I suspected." She grabbed logs from the pile. "Why did I rent her that place?"

"Grandma!" Wesley shouted from the kitchen.

"I'm getting wood." She tested her tone to keep the anger out. "You and Chesley keep on your coats. You're fixing to miss the bus."

"Chesley ain't going today, Grandma."

"You tell him he can't skip another school day and get promoted." Anger re-exploded against the spiraling snow.

"He ain't here." As she came in and spilled the armload of oak onto the floor, he added, "He said he's taking the rifle to shoot him a coyote."

"I know he don't have name brand jeans and fancy sneakers like the Fabers, but he's got to learn that your folks lumping their earnings together can't hardly bring the ends in sight of one another, let alone make them meet. We'll go fetch him."

"The bus went by already. If we ain't there by the time it turns around, we'll miss it."

"All right. I'll park you in the road first."

She hurried him outside, and they skated across the frozen creek and up the incline just as the bus hurtled through the snow screen. But when it wheezed to a stop and the door folded open, Wesley stood immobile with dismay.

"Hop on now. After school you can get off at the garage and ride home with your daddy." Her gaze swung to include the driver. "Joe Earl, when you pass Burns' place this afternoon, you let Wesley off."

Joe Earl prodded the tobacco wad deeper into his cheek with his tongue and lifted an eyebrow in assent.

Wesley glanced back at her frightened as he caught the hand pole and the door huffed shut. The bus jolted to a start.

It pulled away, and she turned from it toward the creek as Chesley appeared on the road to the pasture with a shotgun in one hand.

"Chesley!"

He kept walking, and she didn't shout again but stood and watched until he disappeared into the falling snow.

"I guess it don't matter if a thing's lost in the black of night or in a cauldron of snow," she murmured bitterly. "It's still lost."

Nine

"I didn't get off when I seen the padlock on the door," Wesley bleated happily. "Nobody was at the garage, Grandma, so I didn't get off."

"I guess your daddy went home early because of the snow and all."

"Nobody was there, Chesley, so I didn't get off." He tugged Chesley's arm.

"Yeah, okay." Chesley jerked his sleeve irritably from Wesley's grasp.

Min studied him a second before she asked casually, "You go up by the rent house today while you was out, Chesley?"

But when he didn't look up, she retreated to the kitchen, grabbed a package of ground beef, the color of Teal Endicott's lipstick, and smashed it into the skillet.

While the reek of hot grease filled the kitchen, she dealt plastic place mats onto the table, each mat the laminated photo of a tourist attraction. The Statue of Liberty, the Golden Gate Bridge, Yellowstone's Old Faithful spitting steam into a blue sky.

"Why do you want to keep eating on places none of us'll ever see, Min?" Burns had complained once, and when she'd insisted, "Anything's possible," he'd laughed. "If you believe that, you wait right here while I go get my deed to that property," he'd said, tapping the photographed bridge.

The hamburger sputtered as headlights filled the window and she looked up, her cheeks flushing. "Your daddy's joining us for supper."

But in the next second, the cough of a VW motor replaced the lights, and she corrected, "No, it's your mama."

Footsteps crunched across the snow, and Deborah limped in, still wearing the cheap plastic tam the factory supplied as protection against the copper filings.

"How was work?"

"Like always." She pulled off the plastic mushroom and dropped into a chair.

"Come on, boys."

Min looked at the pus nodules on her daughter's forehead. "Why don't you check out the Campbell Soup plant? That copper dust can't help but be bad for your skin."

"Campbell's ain't hiring."

The boys shoved through the door, and Chesley went to the cupboard, plunked down the ketchup bottle while he looked at his mother and blurted fiercely, "Why can't you fix yourself up? You don't have to look like that all the time, do you?"

Without moving, Deborah appeared to cringe against the chair.

"You don't talk like that to your mama," Min said coldly. "If you don't know how hard she works at that factory, you wait until you get out of school—if you ever do—and then you see about fixing yourself up."

His eyes smoldered like clots of black oil. "I ain't hungry. I'm going home."

As he slammed out, Deborah asked softly, "Can he get home all right?"

"There's a sliver of a moon. He'll be all right." And since her voice sounded calm, neither her daughter or grandson looked up to witness the pain that twisted her lips.

Ten

The next day, Chesley sauntered in, casually holding the chainsaw as if he hadn't stormed from the kitchen the night before. "You need some wood, Grandma?"

"I recollect Faye Landry sniffing chain-saw gasoline and then castrating one of the Robbins' boar hogs."

Chesley laughed. "I ain't aiming to do that, Grandma."

"If you get me wood, I don't want you cutting good oak."

"I ain't aiming to cut live trees neither."

"All right. As long as you stay near me." She followed him outside as the shadow of two hawks skimmed the air like escaping black kites.

He looked up while they walked. "Hawks is sure bold right now."

They reached the curve where Teal Endicott stood unhinging the gate, and Min said softly, "In winter, most everything gets hungry."

Teal dropped the gate in the weeds. "Is this one of your grandsons, Min?"

Chesley gazed at her with no expression.

"I still can't believe you're old enough to have grandsons."

"I had Deborah at fifteen, and she had the twins at fifteen."

Teal gave them a fruit-drop smile. "I see you're off to cut wood. That was so sweet of you to leave me a pile of logs, Min. And those warm antique quilts." She moved off and called gaily to Chesley, "Nice meeting you."

He continued toward the tree line and didn't answer.

Min paused by the fence and said to his back, "You forgot to shut the gate."

He glanced over his shoulder at her. "Grandpa don't have a cow left. He's dying."

"He ain't dead yet, is he?"

"No."

"Then shut the gate."

Eleven

The day after Thanksgiving, Burns burst through the back door. "Min! Stu died this morning. Nolda called and I went up. But he was stone dead. There wasn't a thing anybody could do. The funeral's set for Monday next."

"Even on a weekday there's bound to be a crowd. Stu Hammond was first or second cousin to half the county."

Burns extended slender white fingers, red knuckled with cold, over the wood stove. "He was always proud of how he got the windows in this house air-tight. He said he used to look down from the hill and count every shingle on the roof."

"No one forced Stu Hammond to run off."

He pushed back his dark hair. "Stu waited up there, looking down on his shingles and dying."

"We all got to die, Burns."

He glanced at her. "But there's got to be more to living than this."

Twelve

The hammering pounded so unexpectedly from the front porch that she started.

"How come you didn't hear somebody coming, George?" she said to the dog as she opened the door to a winter sun slanting under the eaves. It was directly behind a woman in a black coat and hat with body fumes crinkling up from her silhouette.

"Can I come in, Min?"

"Nolda?"

The woman stepped inside. "I see you got a new Lazy-Boy."

"I didn't rightly recognize you, Nolda."

Nolda swiveled from the chair to the TV. "And a new rug."

"It's as old as the twins."

Then silence surrounded them under the haze of inky dye before Min finally said, "Is the funeral today?"

"I didn't know if you aimed to come or not."

"I never got around to buying me a black dress. I figured no one'd miss me."

Nolda looked at her, and for a second the teen-aged Nolda glinted through the tired, stone-washed eyes. "I forgave you a long time ago, Min."

Min stood a moment in stunned immobility. "*You* forgave *me*? Did I recollect it wrong? I seem to remember you took off with my husband."

"And I forgave you for letting us go. You could have stopped us."

"Why, I—"

One black sleeve jerked impatiently. "It don't matter. After you took in Burns, Stu couldn't get a cross-eyed look from you. " No glimmer of the early Nolda remained now in the puckered face. "You let Stu and me go off without raising a finger so Stu wouldn't take Burns instead. But I came by to tell you it don't matter. I got over it long ago."

"I know it was a shock for Stu to die and all, but that don't sanction you coming in here and—"

"And I wanted to tell you to start telling the truth about how you felt toward Stu."

Min backed away a step. "No matter how much you're mourning, you got no right to waltz in here and conjecture what feelings Stu Hammond stirred up in me—back then or now."

"Oh, Min. I got every right. You felt nothing but relief when Stu left with me."

She swung the black coat toward the door and shook her head under the old hair and dusty black hat. "And it don't do no good to keep lying. About Stu. Or about Burns."

Thirteen

Nolda had barely gone down the front steps before the twins tumbled in the back door. "Grandma, we're going to a funeral!"

"Mama said to ask if you was riding with us," Chesley said.

"I seen my share of funerals," she stalled. "Remember I also got my cleaning job at the bank."

"First Federal don't give a hoot if you wait until midnight to run that sweeper." He looked at her. "He was my grandpa."

"And he was my husband seventeen years ago. But he ain't either any longer. He's dead." When Chesley's lips thinned, she added, "What I meant, sweetheart, was that—"

"Come on, Wesley. We got to go," Chesley interrupted.

"Tell your folks to come for supper afterward."

Chesley didn't look back. "Nolda said we'd go to McDonald's."

"She don't need to be wasting her money, being a widow and all."

But when the back door slammed, she leveled her stare once more at the front door and the lace curtain behind which Nolda had disappeared. "I was only twenty-eight years old when we got Burns," she said softly. "Maybe it wasn't lying. Maybe it was just something I didn't care to recognize."

Fourteen

Two days later Teal Endicott's red pick-up stopped beside the root cellar, its truck bed crammed with boxes.

"Min!" She climbed down in the incongruous warm winter morning, radiating peaches, raspberries, polished apples. The sun glinted on the blue highlights in her ebony hair. "Min, I hate to do this, but I have to get back to Dallas." House keys swayed from cherry-tipped fingertips. "I know I signed a lease for six months, but something's come up. Of course I want to pay the full amount." She laid a check in Min's palm. "It's been lovely."

"I don't cotton to taking money I didn't earn."

"No, no, it's only fair. You keep it. And thanks for everything." She scuttled from the yard, jumped back into the truck, and her hand vibrated a coral farewell.

"It's a shame you never got to know the kind of man he really was," Min whispered as the little truck pulled away. "I could calculate near to the minute when he was open to discovering Nolda. And I knew right after Stu's funeral that he was aiming to ask you to run off with him."

She watched the pick-up speed across the creek and gun out of sight. "Only someone as guileless as Burns would miscalculate that a few nights under antique quilts meant the same to you as they did to him. Only a man unknowledgeable about women in general would think something more permanent could come from a winter's amusement."

George lumbered from under the house and stopped beside her.

She reached down and fondled his ears, her face tight with relief. "Burns won't be going away after all, George."

Fifteen

"I'll be leaving the end of the week, Min."

Sunset spread plum colored clouds along the horizon, and she stared at him.

"Where you aiming to go?"

"I don't know. Just away from here. I can get work in some garage and then maybe later open my own place."

"You got your own place now. You could expand and maybe—"

"Deborah can file or I will. She can keep the house and the cattle or sell them all. I'll make do with what I get from the garage. I'm going to ask the boys if they want to go with me."

The grass at their feet gloomed to the mauve of ash.

"You know Chesley will want to go. And Wesley does whatever Chesley does."

He nodded.

"You're just feeling low, Burns. What with Stu dropping dead so unexpected and all. Give yourself a few days to perk up and—"

"I figure I'll look into some trade school when I get to where I'm going."

"You're too old for that, Burns. Maybe if Stu hadn't gone off when he did, you could've had a couple of years at the community college, and then—"

"Puckett was saying the other day that guys as old as me go at night to trade schools."

"Puckett can't pour kerosene out of a boot with directions on the heel."

He looked at her. "There's got to be more in life than this, Min."

"Life ain't in the habit of giving us what we fancy."

He nodded again. "But maybe there's something more."

"Maybe there ain't, too."

He flinched.

She waited, then began again, more reasonably. "It just don't seem right you thinking of going off like that so close to Christmas. Why don't you wait at least until you—"

"I need to go now. I wanted you to know first, Min." His green eyes looked at her, and for a brief second in the twilight, they may have contained sympathy.

She instantly averted her gaze. "You sure you have to start over?"

"I can't repair what's broke here, Min."

"I guess you got to do what you think best." Then, "In case you can't sell the garage, you might need some money. I got some uncashed checks."

"I'll be okay."

He raised a hand toward her, but when she continued to stare at the distant hill, he let the hand drop and walked to the truck that had smudged to cordovan sameness in the dusk.

"I'll come by before I go." He hitched himself into the cab, the key clicked, and the engine hummed.

She watched in rigid stillness while the truck plunged into the slate-colored creek, then dripped a fringe of black water like river stones from the tailgate as it lurched up the bank on the other side.

Above the stream, a hawk circled over the cut-paper black of the trees, wheeled, and merged into the darkness.

ACKNOWLEDGEMENTS

"The House on Prytania" was first published in *Embry's Journal*, "A Change in the Weather" in *Cactus Country Anthology, Volume III*, "Twenty-Seven Minutes to Memphis" in *Brain, Child*, "The Settlement" in *The Country and Abroad*, "Wakefield O'Connor" in *Texas Short Stories*, "Arriving on the 7:10" in *The Chariton Review*, "Made in the U. S. A." in *Southern Magazine*, "The Hat'in *Negative Capability*, "Deleting Derek" in *The Country and Abroad*, "The Gold-Leafed Girl" in *The Country and Abroad*, "Hawk Woman at Peterbilt" in *The Georgetown Review*, "The Stand-Off" in *The Griffin*, "Nine Hundred and Thirty Acres" in *Texas Short Fiction: A World in Itself II*, "The Kindness of Strangers" in *The New England Writers Notebook*, "A Night in the Port Authority" in *The Pikeville Review*, "Downward to Darkness" in *The Country and Abroad*

ABOUT THE AUTHOR

Pat Carr has a B.A. and M.A. from Rice, A Ph.D. from Tulane, and eighteen published books, including the Iowa Fiction Prize winner, The Women in the Mirror, and the PEN Book Award finalist, If We Must Die. She's published over a hundred short stories in such places as The Southern Review, Yale Review, and Best American Short Stories.

Her most recent short story collection, The Death of a Confederate Colonel (University of Arkansas Press, 2007), a nominee for the Faulkner Award, won the PEN Southwest Fiction Award, the John Estes Cooke Civil War Fiction Award, and was voted one of the top ten books from university presses for 2007 by Foreword Magazine.

She's won numerous other awards, including a Library of Congress Marc IV, an NEH, the Texas Institute of Letters Short Story Award, an Al Smith Literary Fellowship, a Fondation Ledig-Rowohlt Writing Fellowship in Lausanne, Switzerland, and Arkansas' prestigious 2013 Porter Prize.

She's taught creative writing and literature on graduate and undergraduate levels in numerous universities across the South, has conducted writing workshops from Santa Fe to New York, and in 2011 taught the Civil War novel at New York's Chautauqua Institute. Her writing text, Writing Fiction with Pat Carr appeared from High Hill Press in 2010, and her memoir, One Page at a Time: On a Writing Life, also published in 2010 by Texas Tech University Press, was a finalist for both the Willa Cather Award and the PEN Southwest Non-Fiction Award.

Her most recent fiction, a novella, The Radiance of Fossils, appeared from Main Street Rag Press in 2012. Her graphic novel, Lincoln, Booth, and Me, an examination of the Lincoln assassination from the point of view of Booth's cat, was published by El Amarna Press in the spring of 2013 and was a winner of the 2013 Animal Book Fair Competition.

She lives and writes on a thirty-six acre farm in Arkansas with her writer husband, Duane Carr, three dogs, a cat, and five black chickens. And in case you're curious, the dog in this photo answers to Keats and the chicken is named Emerson.

OTHER BOOKS AND WRITINGS
BY PAT CARR

Lincoln, Booth, and Me: A Graphic Novel of the Assassination by Horatio the Cat as told to Pat Carr (El Amarna Publishing, May 2013)

The Radiance of Fossils (Main Street Rag Press, July 2012)

One Page at a time: On a Writing Life (Texas Tech University Press, December 2010)

Writing Fiction with Pat Carr (High Hill Press, 2010.)

Beneath the Hill (Gray Rabbit Publishing July 16, 2010)

The Death of a Confederate Colonel (University of Arkansas Press, 2007)

Border Ransom (TCU Press, 2006)

If We Must Die: A Novel of Tulsa's 1921 Greenwood Riot (TCU Press, 2002)

Sonahchi A Collection of Myth Tables (Cinco Puntos Press, 1988; 2nd ed. 1995)

Night of the Luminarias (Slough Press, Austin Council for the Arts Award, 1986)

Mimbres Mythology (Texas Western Press, 1979, 1987, 1989)

The Women in the Mirror (Iowa School of Letters Award for Short Fiction) University of Iowa Press (March 1978)

Bernard Shaw (World Dramatists Series) (Frederick Ungar Publishing Co., 1976)

In fine spirits: The Civil War letters of Ras Stirman with historical comments by Pat Carr Washington County Historical Society (1986)